WELCOME TO
Artifice & Access

A DISABILITY IN FANTASY ANTHOLOGY

Stories by: Ashley N. Y. Sheesley | M. Stevenson | Lynne Sargent
Kara Siert | Adie Hart | Harper Kinsley | Natalie Kelda
Rascal Hartley | Casper E. Falls | Zira MacFarlane | Tam Ayers
Elior Haley | Ella T Holmes | Rory G

Edited by: Ella T Holmes

While all of the stories in this anthology value & depict inclusion, please be aware that this book contains the following content that may be difficult for some readers:

One Cream, Five Sugars
• A medical episode (few specific details)

A Witch's Tale
• Battle Trauma (abstracted with few specific details; healing and recovery)

The Changeling of Brushby
• Familial neglect (problematised)
• Changeling lore (problematised)
• Ableism (problematised)
• Arranged marriage

To Make Her Eat
• Missing person
• Consumption of alcohol

Hope, Be It Never so Faint
• Use of weapons (bow and arrows)
• Arranged marriage
• Ableism (problematised)

A Night For Mischief
• Alcohol consumption (on-page)

Lessons in Botany
• Forced isolation (problematised)
• Misgendering (problematised)
• Ableism (problematised)
• Eugenics themes (problematised)

Stroke of Midnight, Shoes of Glass
• Familial neglect/abuse (problematised)

In Another World, I Twist the Knife
• Surgical procedure (on-page; brief; magic)
• Active knife wound (on-page; brief mentions; magic)

The Knife that Makes The Cut
• Death (on-page; drowning)
• Neglect/abuse (mentioned as part of past events)
• Gambling (mentioned as part of past events)

Angharad ferch Truniaw
• War/battle (mentioned as part of past events)

The Girl & The Gum-riddle
• Illness (graphic)
• Ableism (problematised)

City of the Sun
•Ableism (problematised)
• Eugenics themes (problematised)
• Death (mentioned as part of past events)

Foreword

The tale of how this anthology came to be is one I dearly love to begin with 'Once Upon a Time', and quickly follow up with, 'someone was wrong on twitter dot com'. But rest assured, the middle and the end of this tale are lovely. After explaining that disabled and chronically ill people can and should exist in fantasy spaces for the simple reason that we exist in real life, I decided to bite the proverbial arrowhead and shoot my shot at creating an anthology.

I put the call out online, asking if anyone would be interested in submitting or supporting the idea, and the response I got was so heart-warmingly positive that I cried. I received private messages, public replies, and e-mails asking what could be done, how people could help, if there was anything I needed. People have donated time and money to this project, and it is beyond what I could have hoped. The disability community showed up, and I will forever be grateful.

  The goal of this anthology is to say: Disabled and chronically ill people exist. We have stories both realistic and fantastic, and they deserve to be told and shared. In each of the fourteen stories to come, I hope disabled and chronically ill readers see themselves and their experiences, and that they feel welcome. I hope our allies enjoy these new narratives and want more of them. I hope everyone loves them as much as I do.

PLEASE NOTE: In order to preserve authorial voice and style, the English used by each individual contributor has not been changed. As such, you may notice some differences in spelling, punctuation, and language. I have prepared some spares in the event you need them:

Z z " " o ou ' ' s

— Ella T Holmes

Contents

the world
N
E
S
W

One Cream, Five Sugars

— by Harper Kinsley

It starts with a cup of coffee.

Kaida blinks, staring at the ceramic mug before her. A faded ring of
coffee stains the white cup just below the lip, and steam floats from
it in gentle curls. She takes it by the handle, raises it for inspection.
The liquid inside is a creamy brown, the color of mud after a spring
rain, or the hair of her last paramour. Inhaling, Kaida smells comfort.
Her lungs fill with the scent of vanilla and hazelnut and snow on
winter mornings.

Careful to avoid the chip on the porcelain rim, she drinks.

"Long shift again?"

Kaida is no longer hiding in a hayloft, wrapped in nothing but arms
and linen. She is seated at a tavern, her direwolf companion at her feet,
a coffee in her hands, and a woman with light brown skin staring at her
from behind the counter.

Kaida's lips drop into a frown, and she reaches down to dig one
hand in the security of Briarheart's fur, and he nudges against her
leg protectively. A low rumble echoes in his core, not a growl but
a sound of comfort. Similar to the warnings that her heart might
break into an episode, but that's not unusual when she drinks coffee.

He rarely approves of it, but it's one of the few vices Kaida allows herself anymore.

"I don't particularly like my mind being read," she says, regarding the perfectly crafted cup of coffee before her. Dark roast, one cream, five sugars.

The woman gives an exasperated sigh. "I'm not a mind reader, remember? It's the beans that have the magic, not me," she says, shaking her head.

"I don't remember ordering any—"

"You never get anything else," the woman continues. "Doesn't take a mind reader to pick up on habits."

Kaida stops. "I've been here before?"

"Mother Terra help you," the woman sighs. Apparently, she doesn't have any other way of communicating. "Yes. I thought you were playing a prank on me, but you really don't remember, do you?" She drags a hand across her brow, brushing stray, dark hairs back into the loose bun on her head. "Allow me to reintroduce you to the Owl and Sparrow, Feyglen's best all hours dining establishment. I'm Rhia, the sorry wench who's been serving you coffee at godsforsaken hours of the night for the past three weeks without so much as a thank you."

All Kaida remembers is walking into the only establishment open after midnight, eyes bleary and bloodshot, and collapsing into the chair at the counter while her companion curled at her feet. There is not a single memory pointing to this woman before her. But Kaida knows better than to argue with a woman who seems to know more on the subject than Kaida herself—especially one responsible for providing her with coffee.

So she shrugs. Drinks again. Then she nods and says, simply, "Kaida."

"For the Great Three's sakes, I know your name!" Rhia says. It seems she communicates through exhausted half-yelling as well. "You come in here almost every night, order the same damn coffee every time, and accuse me of being a mind-reading sorceress, and every time I tell you, no, I'm just a girl with a magic coffee pot."

"Oh," Kaida says. It feels simple, but there's not really another way to respond. "Well, it's good. Thank you."

"I know it's—wait, did you just say thank you?"

"Yes?" Kaida stares and Rhia stares back. "Do I not normally?"

Rhia shrugs. "If you do, I don't hear it."

Kaida nods, then drinks. "I'll try to bring better manners in the future then."

As she relaxes, Briarheart lays down across her feet once more. She releases him, then grasps the cup with both hands. Her fingers tingle with warmth as it travels through the ceramic to her fingers, which she'd not realized were ice cold until now.

Behind the counter, Rhia idly rubs a cloth over another coffee mug, and for some reason Kaida wonders if this is the third or fourth time she's washed it. "You know, for as many times as you've been here, you've never told me what it is you do that keeps you out this late. Not many people frequenting a small tavern after midnight."

Kaida looks around for some indication of the hour, though all she can see is the darkness outside the dirt-fogged windows. "Not many people running a small tavern after midnight," she responds, instead of just asking for the time.

"I told you, we're the only place open in the middle of the night."

Kaida raises a silver eyebrow. "I thought you said it was the best."

Rhia waves the cup back and forth in a carefree motion. "Same thing, when you think about it."

"Wouldn't that also make it the worst?"

Rhia sighs again. "I suppose it would."

After another long sip, Kaida chuckles. "So, the best, the worst and the only, then. You should be proud of yourself. It takes talent to be three things at once."

"You are so odd," Rhia says.

"Thank you."

"I don't—I didn't—" She throws her hands in the air. "Oh my gods."

Satisfied, Kaida relents. "I'm a mercenary," she says, surprised the arrows on her back, the sword at her side, and the dagger at her waist didn't give it away. "Odd jobs, plundering ruins, the occasional maiming."

The lines in Rhia's face deepen as her face twists into suspicion. "I didn't realize mercs worked this late."

Kaida's laugh is sardonic this time. "Most mercs aren't as desperate as me," she replies, tone a clear indication that's all Rhia will get on the subject.

Taking the hint, Rhia indicates the floor with a short nod. "Is that why you have the dog then?" she asks. "Not that I mind. Didn't even notice him the first few times you brought him in."

"No. Briarheart is a companion," Kaida says, voice taking on a harder quality. She's had to fight for her right to bring him places in the past, even though companions are protected by law. Not that most establishments care when it comes to an animal nearly half the size of their patrons.

As if sensing her discomfort, Briarheart rumbles at Kaida's feet. "Also, he's a direwolf, not a dog," Kaida adds for good measure.

Rhia's face quickly turns to shock, then embarrassment. "Oh—oh, he's a companion," she stammers. "Sorry, I didn't realize—"

"Just don't ask me to move to the corner," Kaida says, only partially joking. Then she unceremoniously downs the rest of the coffee and sets the empty cup on the table before fishing a few coins from her purse. She pushes them forward, an extra coin for good measure. "Here we are."

Rhia swipes the money into her hand and sets the tip aside. "Off already?"

"No rest for the weary," Kaida says as she stands. With each movement, a different joint in her body cracks as her muscles prepare to work once again. "See you around."

"Try to remember me next time you come in," Rhia says.

Kaida grins. "No promises."

*

It is a jar this time, ten days later.

Rhia yelps and drops it when Kaida settles into her customary spot at the counter. Coins rattle against the glass as it falls, but before it hits the ground, Briarheart leaps over the counter and catches it with his jaws the size of an award-winning pumpkin. Kaida laughs when Rhia looks between her and the direwolf, as though asking permission.

"He's trained to catch things whenever my joints give out on me," Kaida explains, and it's enough to prompt the other woman to take the jar back. Secretly, Kaida is surprised Briarheart was so quick to grab it when he usually dislikes picking up anything made of glass. Perhaps he's more concerned with Kaida's potential distress due to the sound, or perhaps he's growing fond of their new acquaintance who's been determined to win him over with bits of dried jerky that she gives to Kaida for when he's off duty.

Rhia continues to stare at Briarheart for just a moment, then glances quickly at Kaida, who gives a short nod with a smirk. He receives a single pat on the head as thanks, then rounds the counter to join Kaida once more. Normally she wouldn't allow others to touch him, but Rhia doesn't ask often, and always asks for permission. Besides, she likes the way Rhia's face lights up and turns the slightest shade of red when she does.

"Good boy," Rhia says, quietly. She stashes the jar on a high shelf behind the counter, then prepares a coffee.

Kaida says nothing, and hides her smile behind a sip when it is handed to her. This one is heavy, and tastes of summer skies and afternoons working the field with her father. Of rougeberries and citrus rinds soaked in brandy. It almost distracts her from the ache in her shoulders, her spine, her hips. "Thank you," she says, unlacing the leather braces around her wrist and thumb. Then she places them on the counter, rotating her stiff hands in small circles.

Leaning forward, Rhia rests her elbows on the counter and considers Kaida for an uncomfortable minute. "If I didn't know better, I'd think your job was starting to wear on you," she says, no doubt wondering why Kaida would take such a physically demanding job when nearly every joint of her body is wrapped, from her whalebone-enforced boots to the clinking rings stabilizing her fingers.

A different face comes to mind when she drinks again. Suddenly, she is very aware of her own heartbeat. "Some of us do what we have to," she says, and punctuates the thought by nodding at the jar. "What's that for?"

Rhia's eyes meet Kaida's and dart away—a look Kaida knows well from seeing it on her younger brother. "It's nothing," she says, predictably.

Rolling her eyes, Kaida scoffs. "When hiding something, the aim is not to be suspicious, you know."

"Not all of us are as artfully dodgy as you."

Kaida's mouth drops open. "I am not dodgy."

"Of course you're not. You just dance around the topic whenever I ask you anything about yourself."

That much is true. In the past few weeks, Kaida has not only remembered Rhia, but almost said too much on more than one occasion. It's too easy to talk to Rhia, with her warmth and her softness and her godsdamned magic coffee.

"It's my escape fund," Rhia admits, so quiet that Kaida isn't sure she heard correctly. "My dream."

Kaida snorts. "Your dream is to run away?"

"It's—I have to." There is a sudden desperation in Rhia's voice. Her fingers grip tighter around a washcloth in her hand. The one she uses to clean coffee mugs when she gets anxious. "I have no future here anymore, not since… it's just me now, and… there must be somewhere I can start over."

"That's what you work this late for?"

Rhia is strangling the cloth now. "Yes."

A long beat of silence passes between them, a precipice between one thing and the next. Kaida takes a slow drink. "Why do we run ourselves ragged for the sake of the things we want most?" she asks at last, shaking her head.

That familiar sigh escapes Rhia. "I suppose that's just being alive."

*

Kaida keeps coming back.

The jar fills.

Her heart aches, in more ways than one.

The coffee tastes of sweetness and bitterness. Of sleepless nights and fields of clover, of hope in something on the horizon and regret of what was let go.

One cream, five sugars.

And one night, it tastes of Rhia's lips.

*

The cup shatters on the ground as it slips from Rhia's grasp.

Kaida doesn't see it, just hears it as she drags herself to the counter, weary and on the verge of collapse. Her muscles scream, her bones creak, blood pounds in her ears. Briarheart whimpers as he circles her, glancing between her and Rhia as though begging the other woman to do something.

"What in Great Valis' name is wrong with you?" Rhia asks, looking unsure of what to do. Kaida's never been this bad before.

Kaida gives the best smile she can muster. "Coffee," she manages. "One cream, five—"

"You want coffee? At a time like this?" Rhia demands. "Look at yourself!"

In response, Kaida shrugs. "It's not like I get to choose my jobs," she says, even if that's not quite true. "I take whatever pays the most." A tingling begins in her fingers, and she removes the brace on her left hand to free the circulation. By doing so, she reveals the bruising on her arms, which only serves to make Rhia more frantic.

"Maybe you should switch careers," she says, and her tone lacks its usual mirth. "Killing yourself slowly can't be worth whatever it is you're working for."

"What's a few bruises every now and then?" Kaida asks with a wry smile. "Can I get that coffee now?"

Rhia shakes her head. "Insufferable." But she turns to prepare Kaida's drink all the same.

It isn't the same coffee—Kaida knows immediately. This has a subtler, yet more bitter flavor. Something sharp and warm, like cinnamon and mint. She thinks of an embrace after a long day, a sincere apology. Of her longing to feel Rhia's lips once again. The tingling intensifies, something that's usually a warning sign for Kaida, but when she looks at her arms, the mottled splotching has started to disappear.

Magic coffee indeed.

Before she can take another sip, she is interrupted by Rhia's fretting. She rounds the counter and reaches out, hesitating. "Are you… hurt anywhere else?"

"Might have some nicks. I think something got my left side," Kaida admits.

Quietly, Rhia asks, "May I?"

Kaida nods.

Rhia's thumbs are soft against Kaida's pale skin, examining her arms, her neck, her face. Kaida wishes Rhia would take her face in those soft hands, pull it closer to her. Instead, she removes the leather pauldrons from Kaida's shoulders, carefully and modestly assessing Kaida's body for other injury.

It is too late when Kaida realizes she should have told Rhia to stop.

Rhia pauses. She whispers, "What is this?"

Kaida's breathing shallows as Rhia's fingers pass over the puckered, silvery skin over the left side of Kaida's pale chest. Heat and cold tingle on the surface of her skin. Underneath, she feels the aortic valve made of willowheart beating in her chest, much faster than it should be.

Kaida's guard slips, clattering to the floor like Rhia's coffee cup. She hates this. Hates her vulnerability, her weakness. Hates that at a time like this, all she wants is to kiss Rhia until she feels nothing else.

Rhia asks again. "What happened to you?"

"I was born with a broken heart." She tries to laugh it off. She coughs instead.

"Kaida."

And finally, Kaida finally spits out the name to her suffering. "Nafram's Disease." The curse that despite her persistent prayers to the Great Three, not Valis, not Falo, not even Mother Terra deemed it worthy to lift from her. "It's… You've probably never heard of it. We didn't know until… well, my…" She sees her mother, belly full, and rosy cheeked. Then she is ghostly pale, lying in a casket with flowers in her hair. "If we hadn't replaced parts of my heart, I…" Her mind wanders as she thinks of the disease, the things that it's stolen from her.

"I don't know it," Rhia admits. "But… Kaida, you shouldn't be… I can't imagine fighting is healthy for you if—"

"You have a dream?" Kaida interrupts, and it is a question and a reminder at the same time. "I have a brother. With a broken heart." She balls her fists. "The elves have created… alternatives. Magical pieces that can keep the body running how it should, but…" A fist lands on the table and Kaida realizes it's hers. Kaida meets Rhia's eyes. "Do you understand how much that costs? Especially for a poor farming family with one income? I don't do this because I want to, or because it's safe. I do it because it's the fastest way to save him before his heart gives out on him too."

Silence hangs in the air.

Kaida destroys herself inside—kicks and screams and throws herself, knowing that she shouldn't have said anything to this woman. Rhia knows nothing about this, has no reason to care. It is Kaida's burden to carry, with her father sick and barely able to provide for their daily needs, and her brother Hale half-blind and far more affected by the disease than Kaida. It's just being alive, knowing that you would work yourself to death to save someone who mattered to you.

Rhia opens her mouth to say something—

Then screams Kaida's name instead.

Pain explodes in the left side of Kaida's chest, tearing her apart in two. It shoots through her back, her neck, her skull, through her panic as she wonders if she should have prayed harder to the gods. She hears Briarheart yelping, nuzzling into her hand as she grips his fur. A deafening trill echoes in her ears and her fingers fill with needles.

She drops to the floor.

And then there is nothing.

*

The jar is empty.

Just as empty as the tavern in the morning. A few customers sit scattered throughout the dining area, an individual with a broadsword tucked into the corner by the table they sit at, a cloaked woman reading a book while sipping a tea, a man with a newspaper near the window at the front. They don't understand how they intrude on a space that belongs to someone else, the privilege it is to be in this establishment.

And yet, when Kaida sits down, it all seems to fade away.

"I hear this place is open at some godsforsaken hours of the night," she says to the woman behind the counter.

Rhia turns, and for a moment she can only stare.

"But I also hear the coffee is pretty good," Kaida continues.

After a moment, she asks, "One cream, five sugars?"

"You know what I like."

Rhia slowly sets about making the drink. An age passes before she places it in front of Kaida and says, "They weren't sure you'd make it."

"Willowheart isn't called the 'elven secret' for nothing," Kaida answers. "And they found traces of some enchanted mixture in my blood. Something about healing properties, something magic… Whatever it is, it slowed down the dissection and kept me here long enough for the clerics to do their thing." A knowing look crosses her face. "But you wouldn't know anything about that."

"I'm just a girl with enchanted beans," Rhia says, shrugging.

Kaida takes a long drink, letting the taste fill her entire being. It smells of fresh spring mornings, and tastes like the last of the winter cold melting away. Just as she opens her mouth to compliment it, Rhia drops a leather pouch on the counter. Warily, Kaida stares at it. "What's this?" she asks.

When she looks inside, Kaida immediately pushes it away. "I can't take this," she says, shaking her head.

"You don't have to, but if… Kaida, I care about you," Rhia says, cheeks turning a shade redder. "If this… Would it help?"

The amount of coin in the satchel is enough not only to purchase the replacement, but to cover the entire procedure from a respectable physician. They might even be able to afford the eye procedure they've put off as well.

But Kaida can't take this gift.

"Rhia, I can't—"

"Pay me back then, if you want to," Rhia insists. "But you shouldn't have to work yourself nearly to death. Maybe someday we'll live in a world that cares more for the health of its people. But for now, if I can help, let me do that."

Tears prick at the corner of Kaida's eyes. "You don't understand," she says. "If you give me this, you might never see me again."

"Oh sure, take my money and—"

"My family lives on the other side of the continent."

That gives Rhia pause. The mirth immediately drains from her face. "You mean you'd have to leave?"

Kaida nods. "Not to mention we'll have to go away to the elves, and I'll have to help with the recovery process. It's… there's a lot to it." She reaches down to place a hand on Briarheart, as though he can give her the strength to leave. "I don't know if I'll ever see you again."

"Maybe," Rhia agrees, "but I know I'll regret it more if I don't do this."

They stare at each other, so many unspoken words passing between them. Things they both wish they'd said, things they wish they'd done differently.

In the end, Kaida takes the pouch.

"I swear I'll be back," she says softly, swallowing back the lump in her throat.

"Who knows?" Rhia asks, a smile on her lips. "Maybe I'll find you first."

Harper Kinsley

Harper is an ace, disabled author who has been writing since she could hold a pencil. She loves to write empowering stories of hope for those who might feel otherwise alone, and hopes others will feel an honest comfort when they read her work. In addition to writing, Harper is also a part-time educator and full-time DM who lives with her partner and their cat in the Midwestern United States.

"I have a number of disabilities, but the one I chose specifically to write about in this story is a rare genetic disorder called Marfan Syndrome. The main character's disorder — "Nafram" which is Marfan backwards — is a connective tissue disorder that effects the heart, lungs, eyes, joints, and also results in hypermobility.
To date, I have only found two fiction books that mention this disease, and I hope that by writing about it, I can spread awareness and help others feel less alone."

A Witch's Tale

— by Rascal Hartley

There once was a witch who could cure almost anything.

She had a name, as most witches do, and she lived in the woods, as all witches do. She liked sunlight dappling through green leaves overhead, and she liked the thing shaped like a cat that would sit on her windowsill and purr. She liked embroidering her skirts and decorating her cane with crystals and pinecones. But, most of all, she liked the heroes that came through.

They didn't come through often, as heroes are not an everyday sort of thing, but at least twice a decade, some knight or another would invariably knock on her door and ask for shelter. On the few occasions they made it back, she healed their wounds and sent them on their way. She liked being a footnote in their stories, a fond remembrance. *And I was healed by Lady Golgora, may peace rest fondly with her.*

She healed broken bones and sprained ankles, arrow pokes and upset stomachs. She strained willow bark for headaches and harvested passionflower for ill memories. She knew how to cure the mumps, measles, mouth sores, and mange. There is but one thing that she could not heal, and when she opens her door one late fall evening, it finds her.

A knight looks up. The helmet hides under the knight's arm, and their eyes are wide and pleading. They're far too young to be here.

"Lady Golgora," the girl pleads, dropping to a knee with a wince, "I beg that you might heal me."

Lady Golgora frowns, kneeling to be level with the very young knight. "What ails you, my child?"

The girl squeezes her eyes shut. "I fought Ankorika, the great dragon." Her head drops. "I failed and had to retreat. He…" She hesitates, then unstraps her breastplate and guards, revealing scarred burns all along her chest and right arm.

"Oh," Lady Golgora whispers, "my dear. I am so sorry. Dragon fire cannot be healed."

The girl finally meets her gaze, proud brow furrowed. "But I've heard your tales. They say you can cure anything. You *are* the Lady Golgora, are you not?"

"I am, but I have said what I said. I cannot heal you. No one can."

The girl looks at her burned arm, eyes unseeing. "I cannot feel it. I cannot move it."

"I know. It will get better in time, but it will never heal. I can give you something for the horrible head pain I'm sure you have. Come inside." She straightens with much effort, leaning heavily against the doorframe.

The girl follows hesitantly, armor still on the doorstep. She says nothing.

"You will need a new tunic as well. Yours is in ruins."

The girl swallows. "What do I do?"

"Drink this." Lady Golgora hands over a cup of sweet-smelling medicine.

"I am a *knight,*" the girl protests, eyes stinging. "What do I *do?*"

"You rest for now."

"My arm! What do I do about my arm?!"

Lady Golgora gives her a tight smile. "You rest for now," she repeats. "I cannot heal you, as I have said. It will take time before anything changes, and even then, it will never be the same. This is it now."

"How do you know?" she pleads, tears brimming. "Surely even you cannot know everything."

The witch pulls up her skirt, revealing a mangled and scarred leg. "Believe me, child: if it could be healed, I'd know."

"I'm a *knight,*" the girl repeats like that will change fate, like the world has ever cared for the plans of humans.

"And for now, you are a knight resting in my home. I have a guest bedroom. It is yours now."

The girl says nothing else, just stares at her charred hand, and Lady Golgora stokes the fire as the knight mourns.

*

The knight does not reveal her name until the third day, when Lady Golgora is brewing a breakfast tea and waiting on nettle scones to bake. The girl trudges slowly into the kitchen, eyes puffy, borrowed tunic hanging down to her knees, and says, "Arelis. My name is Arelis. You are owed that much."

"I am owed nothing," Lady Golgora responds, pouring two cups. "Please, sit. You've eaten almost nothing."

"I don't feel hungry." Still, Arelis sits and blows gently on the tea.

"Do you have someone waiting for you at home? You can send a letter."

Arelis looks suddenly again at her right arm, face anguished.

"I can write it for you."

"No one awaits me," Arelis finally says. "There is no need."

"How did such a young one as you end up a knight?"

"I'm seventeen," Arelis bites back, then sighs. "The kingdom is getting desperate."

"I see. I'm sorry."

She sniffs miserably and takes a sip of her tea. "I thought I could handle the dragon myself."

"You ran off, then."

Arelis winces. "I thought… I had trained my whole life. I was *ready.*"

"No one is ever ready for dragons, my dear." Lady Golgora pulls the scones from the oven and sets one before Arelis. "It will be hot."

Arelis stares at her as she makes her slow way around the cottage. "Can you move your leg? It seems like you can."

"Some. It is not easy. Some days are easier than others."

"Then why can I not move my arm?"

"Because it's only been a few days, little knight. Be patient."

"When can I fight dragons again?" Lady Golgora says nothing, so Arelis presses on. "I deserve *revenge.*"

"You do," Lady Golgora agrees slowly. "Let us focus on getting your arm at least moving first."

Arelis sighs but accepts the instructions, munching idly on her scone as the birds sing something somber outside.

On the eighth day, Lady Golgora is picking herbs from her garden as Arelis sits on a stone bench, face turned towards the sun. Her eyes are closed and her brow furrowed. "I am thinking," she says, "of what I did wrong. How I could have avoided my fate."

"And what are you discovering?"

"I don't know yet. But it can't have been for nothing. I have to learn from it." She falls silent a while longer. "Perhaps humility," Arelis finally says, quieter. "Perhaps caution."

"No," Lady Golgora tells her plainly, dusting her dirty hands off on her apron. "Those are not it."

"How can you be so sure? There is some lesson I had to learn. That is why I am here. That is why I—" She sighs. "That is why I have been hurt."

Lady Golgora picks a bouquet of lavender and passionflower, then stands and gives it to the young girl with sad eyes. "No," she repeats gently. "There are other ways to learn those lessons. It did not have to hurt."

"Then why did it?!" Arelis shouts, then winces and curls in on herself. "I'm sorry."

Lady Golgora kisses her forehead sweetly and brushes her hair from her eyes. "There is no lesson to learn," she tells the girl gently. "This is not the work of fate."

"Then what is it the work of?" Arelis asks, voice stained with tears.

"A dragon," the witch responds kindly, then goes back to gathering her herbs.

Sometime in the second month, Arelis moves one finger. The joy she wants to feel is drowned in the pain of it, and as Lady Golgora sits beside her on the overstuffed couch, Arelis hides her face in her apron and sobs.

"It isn't fair!" she cries, good hand gripping folds of mended fabric.

"I know," the witch responds, brushing a gentle hand across tangled hair.

"I wish I had known. I wish someone had told me before."

"I know," the witch says again, pressing a kiss to brown hair.

"I missed my last good day," Arelis tells her like a confession, an echo of desperation kept in a wardrobe in the corner of her heart. "I missed it and I didn't even know."

"I know," the witch repeats, holding her as tightly as she dares. "I went through it, too. I know, little knight. I know."

"How did you survive it? How did you learn to live like this?"

"Would you like me to show you?"

"Please. Please."

The next morning, Lady Golgora teaches Arelis to bake bread.

It is not perfect: she cannot knead it as she wishes to, and she grows weary far sooner than she once did, but Lady Golgora puts it in the oven regardless, and it is served with warm butter and rhubarb jam.

"You did well," the witch tells her, and Arelis sniffs as she looks at the bread.

"I did terribly."

"But you did it, didn't you?"

The next day Arelis picks herbs with Lady Golgora, and though she grits her teeth, she manages to pick some with her right hand.

"It hurts too much to do." Arelis hangs her head.

"Then don't do it," the Lady replies, and picks them for her.

The next evening, Arelis draws her own bath, though the witch offers to do it for her, and she lies in the warm water and stares at the ceiling, at war with herself. When she emerges, she stands before the Lady Golgora, hair dripping wet.

"I cannot kill dragons anymore, can I?" It is not a question, not really.

The Lady puts her embroidery down, thinking. "What do *you* say?"

"I say I cannot move without hurting anymore. I say simple tasks are difficult. I say my life has changed and I cannot go back to who I was."

"That's true," the Lady acquiesces.

"So I cannot kill dragons anymore."

The Lady hums and picks her embroidery back up. "Goodnight, Arelis."

Arelis bows her head, but casts back one odd glance before leaving the room.

At the start of summer, after the leaves have died only to bud anew, Arelis picks up her sword.

She does nothing with it, merely holds it in her left hand and stares at its dull shine, the engravings that had been carved so long ago, in another life. They stare back at her, waiting.

She uses it to chop down vines covering the trees around the garden.

The days become easier, as time makes all days, and Arelis becomes skilled in the art of difference. She learns how to do things with her better side, how to avoid moving her right arm too much, how to soothe it quicker when she forgets. She learns how to make balms and medicines, and when another hero comes through on his way to save some princess or another, she tries not to stare at how easily he moves.

It is once again fall, nearly a year after she showed up on Lady Golgora's doorstep, when she turns to the witch and asks again, more hesitantly, "I cannot kill dragons anymore, can I?"

The Lady's eyes sparkle, and Arelis feels something in her heart take hold of her. "What do you say?"

"I say I am better at moving without hurting. I say simple tasks must be modified, and I am good at doing so. I say my life has changed and I cannot go back to who I was."

"That's true," the Lady replies.

"So I cannot kill dragons as I once did. I have to change it."

"You do," the Lady whispers with a wide smile.

"And I might die."

"You might."

"I might fail."

"That is a possibility. Who are you doing this for?"

"For me," Arelis responds immediately, with conviction. "For no one else. I deserve revenge."

"You do."

"Will you train me?"

"It has been long since I have fought, my child, but yes. As well as I can."

And so, when the first leaves begin to clutter the ground, Arelis once again puts on her armor.

She is clumsier than she once was, and she cannot use a shield, but as the leaves turn and the snow falls soft and heavy, Arelis manages to fight off trees and vines, scarecrows and flowers. She winces into the cottage every evening, where the witch brews her a soothing tea every night. They fall into a rhythm until the snow begins to melt, and restlessness enters Arelis's bones.

"I think I must leave soon," she says over breakfast, cottage cheese and oats and strawberries dripping with honey. "I'll lose my nerve if I wait any longer."

"Then we shall pack together. Remember you must take many rests."

"I know, mother hen," Arelis teases back, and after breakfast they fill her pack with many foods and herbs, medicines and poultices. Lady Golgora reads her stories of brave heroes that night, heroes of whom she is but a footnote. Arelis falls asleep with her head in the witch's lap.

She leaves with the dawn, and the birds and the bugs and even the thing shaped like a cat bid her goodbye. She turns, once, to wave one final time at Lady Golgora, who stands in her garden with grasses caressing her ankles, and disappears over the hill.

There once was a witch who could cure almost anything.

She had a name, as most witches do, and she lived in the woods, as all witches do. She liked laughing with a knight she sometimes called her daughter, and she liked the thing shaped like a cat that kept staring at the now-empty room. She liked patching smaller skirts and decorating her cane with paintings of knights, and she liked singing duets late into the afternoon. But, most of all, she liked the heroes that came through.

They didn't come through often, as heroes are not an everyday sort of thing, but once a knight had knocked on her door and asked for a home, for understanding, for family, and she, unknowingly, had accepted. On the few occasions a hero made it back, she healed their wounds and sent them on their way, and always, she mourned the loss. She had once liked being a footnote in their stories, a fond remembrance, but now finds it remarkably lonely. *And I was taken in by Lady Golgora, may her dreams be fond ones of me.*

She healed broken hearts and sprained feelings, tear tracks and upset frowns. She strained willow bark for headaches and harvested passionflower for afternoon tea. She knew how to cure sadness and heartache, knew the pain of fate's cruelty. There is but one thing that she could not heal, and when she opens her door this late spring morning, it finds her once more.

A knight looks up at her. The helmet is under the knight's arm. The right leg is favored over the left. The eyes she knows from fond dreams.

"Mother hen," Arelis says with a smile, though it pains her to do so. "I've heard you can cure almost anything."

Lady Golgora pulls Arelis into a tight hug that is followed by many apologies, and the knight laughs and leans hard against the doorframe.

"May I come in?" she asks, and the witch is already preparing her a seat and a salve.

"I was terrified for you," the Lady admits with trembling hands as she attempts to soothe burns across leg and stomach and face.

"So was I," Arelis replies. "I almost didn't make it." She catches the Lady's wrist and pauses her to lean their foreheads together. "I did it, mother hen. I killed Ankorika, the great dragon. I told him it was for you."

And the Lady Golgora cries and holds her child once more, shaking and joyous and relieved. They share a supper of roasted roots and fresh berries and flavorful greens, and they make blueberry scones and sip tea late into the night, until the Lady convinces Arelis to finally go to bed. Even then, Arelis does not immediately lie in the sheets that smell of lavender. She sits in the yellow chair and leans her head back and smiles, even as tears fall down her cheeks. She is *home*.

The next morning brings more medicine and an aching head and shaking body, and Arelis remains in her bed as the witch brings her food and water and gentle stories. Arelis gives her the dragon's tooth, which she hangs in a place of prominence over their mantle.

It is a month this time before she can get out of bed, and yet another before she trusts herself enough to attempt walking again, even with the cane the Lady has carved her. On it is a painting in forest shades of Arelis slaying the dragon. Love wells up in her heart.

When the seasons have changed twice, Arelis finds her place on the stone bench outside while her mother tends to the garden and brings her vegetables and fruit to try. The thing that looks like a cat curls contentedly in her lap.

"Where after this time?" the Lady asks as she hands over a forked carrot. "What plans does the great Arelis have?"

"I think I am quite done with plans, mother hen," Arelis returns gently. "I think I have done all I will do. If you are so inclined, though, I have found myself somewhat interested in medicine. If you would teach me, train me."

"An apprentice?"

"If you'll have me."

"I'd love nothing more," Lady Golgora answers with a smile, and the birds sing something joyous.

There once were two witches who could cure almost anything.

They had names, as most witches do, and they lived in the woods, as all witches do. They liked singing songs in the early morning light together, and they liked the thing shaped like a cat that they named, fondly, Ankorika. They liked embroidering their skirts and decorating their canes with crystals and pinecones, and they liked supper and tea and long afternoons by the brook. But, most of all, they liked the heroes that came through.

They didn't come through often, as heroes are not an everyday sort of thing, but once upon a time, a knight had knocked on the eldest's door to ask for a home, for understanding, for family. They found these things in each other, and were inseparable after. They were no longer merely a footnote in stories, some fond remembrance. They were the pages. They were the story.

They healed broken bones and sprained ankles, arrow pokes and upset stomachs. They strained willow bark for headaches and harvested mint for afternoon tea. They knew how to cure sadness and heartache, how to find happiness in each other, in knowing they were not alone. There was but one thing that neither could heal, and every morning, they stared down the burns on the skin of each other, sat down, and had delicious tea. And if either had been asked how the story would end, years ago, they would have said *heartache*. They would have said *ruin*.

As it is, this story ends thusly: and they lived happily ever after.

Rascal Hartley

Rascal Hartley is from the southern United States, and when they aren't busy binding books or collecting various bones, you can find them curled up in their favorite chair, writing. Their favorite author is a tie between Jack Kerouac and J.R.R. Tolkien, but the book they re-read every year is The Last Unicorn.

"Where are we?" — I asked my small group of friends that months ago, when looking for books with disability representation like us. The moment it came into my head, it wouldn't leave. "Where are we?" I love fantasy, and, when I was younger, I loved to make up stories with people like my friends as the heroes. "Where are we?" Now, older, with different friends (because, as I'm sure we all know, disability changes more than your accessories), I find myself looking for us in fantasy books and not finding anything.
I love my friends more than the world, and it's not fair that they don't get to see themselves in the pages of our favorite books. "Where are we?" Easy: right here. I wrote us right here. Ari, Holly, Jess— this one's for you. I wrote this for you. We're right here.

Use Your Words

— *by Zira MacFarlane*

Author's Note: Budgie is a character who cannot speak due to physical trauma. He has been written as an exploration of my own selective mutism and the barriers that I've had to work to overcome in a career that is not friendly to a lack of speech.

As such, Budgie (much like myself) learned to sign much later in life than many folks who use it and with no formal education. I've transcribed how I craft sentences in sign, a somewhat messy mixture of American, British, and home. The grammar does differ strongly from the English I've transliterated into, and this replicates how the words flow through my head when I'm translating my thoughts into signs. For clarity, I have formatted sentences that have been signed with quotation marks **and** italics.

"Spoken words."

"Signed words."

Enjoy the piece! Budgie is a character very close to my heart.

Damn it. Why isn't the ward failing?

The thief's heart raced as he quickened his art in the darkness, his hands flicking from tool to tool, planting an increasingly intricate pattern of gemstone-tipped needles around the chest's lock. He paused for a moment, swiping a sweat-sodden spike of hair out of his eyes, watching the flares from each pinpoint burn against the scintillating strands of magic's web splayed out across the lock's metal filigree. But still it held.

Not enough? More would burn a hole through floor and roof. A low, forced chuckle. *Hardly subtle.*

And then came the voice, a familiar lilt perfectly tuned to turn his blood to ice. "Budgie, darling, I know this is your handiwork." A soft creak at the top of the stairs, a rattle at the door. "I know your little shadowmist jars when I smell them. And I know this job isn't guild approved."

Jackdaw. A caveling. The dark won't slow him, not one bit.

He tapped at the facets of a large crystal housed in a pouch at his hip, tried to slow the beating of his heart.

Thank Web and Weft that I chained the handle. Should give me a few more moments.

He drove another needle into the chest's lock. The ruby tip blazed. Budgie's breath caught, hair on his arms rising as the ward's web sent sympathetic shivers over his skin, the ley lines snarling around the barbed point. Then, with a sickening crack, the needle broke. Unbound magic whipped past him, scoring a burning trail across his hands. He opened his mouth, searching for any way to sever the leylines, any trick that could be done in silence.

But there was none. Budgie grunted hoarsely, panic once more squeezing a more rapid rhythm from his heart. A deafening crack spooked him further still, jumping halfway out of his hide, pain flaring bright as wooden splinters from the now-shattered door peppered his skin. Out of the corner of his eye, he saw Jackdaw saunter into the attic, merrily spinning shadows around his hand – deadlier than knives to one of his training.

No chance to fight. Only flight left.

He dragged his final ace from a pouch. The crystal, warm with the light of tightly wound magic. And he shattered it, the blast of light just enough to cover his slip through a window into the night, hounded by Jackdaw's muffled curses and tense laughter.

*

Pain…

Budgie gritted his teeth, staring down at the parts on his work bench. He'd run from green copper rooftops to cobblestone alleys, trying to escape the searching gaze of Jackdaw's shadowy familiars. He'd even had to duck under the foul water of one of the shipping canals, left breathing through a reed. The burns on his hands were already puffing up, red and weeping.

He tried to drag plans together, organize the chaos of his thoughts, but nothing came. Perhaps more accurately, everything came. A haze of ideas, of links, the Web of magic reflected in the web of his own thoughts. With each concept probed, a hundred twitched in return. He groaned.

First, the wounds. Second, the focus.

The cabinet of alchemicals was always well stocked. He looked at the cleansing herbs, the bandages, the teas. Not for the first time, a thought slunk through his head.

If I could speak… If I could harness magic with my voice, I could mend my hands myself.

I could have broken that lock. Used exactly the right amount of force. No backlash.

If I had a voice.

He paused, rinsing his hands in a stinging solution, the acidic scent of pine filling his nostrils.

*Why does it have to be **my** voice?*

There's an idea. He grinned, darting back to his bench. Grabbed papers and charcoal. And he began to sketch. The light of day rose, then fell. Budgie barely moved from where he sat.

*

Cool, thin hands dragged him from his work trance, gently squeezing his shoulders. He suppressed a grumble at the interruption, instead leaning back into their owner's embrace. After all, he'd asked them to come.

"Budgerigar. How goes it?" The hands left his shoulders, the tap of boot-heels on cold stone echoing as the presence stepped back.

And he turned to face Cay, his partner in love, laboratory, and crime. Grinned. His hands flashed through a series of signs, starting with the sign-name he'd given them. *"Coruscation! Slow. Many difficulties. Make for much fun."*

Caylyx sighed, a hint of an indulgent smile flitting over their heather lips. They were squinting, their dusk-grey eyes ill suited to the glare of the crystalline lights Budgie used to light his lab, their button nose scrunched upwards. They wove words with sign, still a student in the unfamiliar language. "You never like things that are simple, do you?" *"What challenges? You not moving?"*

Budgie stuck his tongue out in mock offence, hands crafting a response. *"Simple too boring."* Then let his face perk up. *"Found battery-crystal. Found leylines in copper and steel. Made strings for voice box..."* And let it fall. *"Just need voice."*

Cal chuckled, shaking their head, their loose silvery hair glittering in the harsh light.

Budgie's head thrummed, thoughts bubbling to the surface. *Gorgeous. Flashes of brilliance every time they move. And every time they speak. Coruscation.*

"You are still a brat, Budgerigar." Cay closed their eyes now, resting them from the glare.

Cave light, never as bright as the stars above. Only ever borrowed light. But how to borrow sight? Budgie frowned, the new problem tickling at their mind. For a moment, they were taken back to where they'd met.

*

The caverns under the Mountain had been darker than any surface night. Without sunstones and foxfire guidestones, travellers were at the mercy of their other senses. The endless rustling of the Mycelial Caul Forests, their roots moving without wind; the thick scents of earth and stone and breaking water. The torturous relief that the odd breeze brought to the stuffy dull heat. Budgie had loved it.
The webs of magic were untamed down there, leylines so thick that they formed mats across the landscape. Budgie's eyes were unaccustomed to the dark, but the air had glowed with power, and he had been so very excited to harness it. Perhaps too excited.

A younger Caylyx had tackled him away from a particularly gorgeous concentration of Ironblood Rocks. It had turned out that a deep enough pooling of magic would sometimes "catch" emotions. Fall sick with them. His own curiosity had been reflected in the target of his research, and it had been preparing to discover his own inner workings. They had fled from its newfound life together, Caylyx throwing fire, Budgie throwing thunderstone, driving back questing hands of stone until they had long left the rock wraith behind.

42

They had lain together in a bed of whispering roots after, laughing so hard they could not walk. The young caveling had offered to guide him after that, and they had traveled together since.

*

A sharp tap on his forehead brought Budgie back to the present. Caylyx was frowning, almost worried. "You were so far away. Where did your mind take you?"

He clicked his tongue. *Don't like falling that far into reverie in front of them. It's getting worse again.* "Best memory. When I met you."

They chuckled. "Flatterer." The blood had risen in their cheeks, causing them to blush a pleasant heather. "I am glad to be a part of your happier hours." Then, cocking their head, they succumbed to their own curiosity. "A voice?" "*Why you need voice?*"

Budgie screwed up his face, frustration at the challenge seeping through. He jerked his thumb outward from under his chin, then moved the flat of his hand over his other fist. *"Not enough. Not good enough. Not flexible enough."* He frowned. *"Too much pressure? My magic breaks."*

"Ah, that job from two nights past, it went poorly?" Caylyx reached out, their heavily lidded eyes sympathetic as they ruffled Budgie's mohawk. They paused, running their thumb over the shorn hair below it. "That's an even six failures out of a dozen jobs."

Budgie rolled their eyes. *"Still here. Not been caught yet. Not say that's a failure."*

"And what happens if you are? Work is not easy for us in this city. How would I pay the wergild that your freedom would demand? Or would you prefer us both to rot, far away from one another?"

The pair sat facing each other. Budgie scowling, Caylyx's expression neutral. He ducked away from their hand. Began to sign.
Too fast. Too full of feelings. Calm down, or they won't understand.

"How will we ever do better? If we are too afraid to forge a future?"
He took a breath, swept a hand across his face, trying to steady his
expression and mask the hurt, the fear behind his eyes.

But he saw the recognition on Cay's face. Saw them bite their lip, a
certain tinge of sorrow flavoring their brow. They both stayed silent for
a moment, Budgie huddled in on himself, Caylyx hovering.

Budgie swallowed. *"Sorry. High feelings. Not your fault."*

Caylyx nodded, taking his hand in theirs. They sighed, setting their
jaw. "Well, if you are determined, how might we find you a voice?"
Seeing his eyebrows raised in surprise, his mouth hanging slack, they
laughed. "I know you. You will find a way, with my help or with none.
And, so, I do believe that I shall follow the intrigue. Indulge me."

Budgie smiled slyly. *"Maybe you not approve."* He flourished,
waving his hand over a spectrum of colored crystals strewn across
papers and brass plates on his work table. Each shard was lit faintly
by a glow hidden within. *"Once I only stole treasures. But over the
last few jobs I stole voices too!"* Cay blinked slowly, the plan starting
to reveal itself. Budgie could see them re-analyzing the last few risks
that they had gently chided him on and he dissolved into giggles. He
tapped each fragment in turn. *"I am a thief to other thieves! But I must
be opportunistic. I still not have a full voice."* A grimace. *"I not have
time to take full lexicon of Jackdaw. And I had to break holding crystal
to escape."*

His partner sighed, chuckling lightly. "Oh Budgerigar, I do know that
you like things to be poetic. But perhaps for your last shard, could you
accept a gift?" They looked into his eyes, smiling. "May I be part of
your voice?"

It was Budgie's turn to blush. He nodded.

"Very well." Caylyx took up a purple crystal from the workbench
and began to sing slowly, suffusing it with magic. Budgie watched,

mouth slightly open, entranced by the layers of his lover's voice.
Each shift in pitch and word drew the leylines of the crystal tighter,
drew an intricate pattern, a spider spinning a silken web into a taut
net surrounding the words that had been freely given to him. The final
shard lay flawless, its surface glittering, suffused with Caylyx and
coruscating more beautifully than any of its companions.

As the song ended, Caylyx slumped down against Budgie. "That..
was a lot. Let me catch my breath." They peered over at the largest
open scroll, pinned against cork above the bench, studying the sketch
and the parts. "A bird, that's certainly thematic. What do you plan to
call it?"

Budgie's fingers spelt out the name he'd chosen. *"L-A-R-A.
Guess why!"*

Caylyx groaned. "Larynx. It's short for larynx, isn't it." They smiled
at him, resting their head against his chest. "Never change."

*

Budgie finished slotting the last of the fragments into carefully
crafted slots ringing Lara's heart and throat. He'd barely breathed
in the final stages, each wire and each gear needing to be placed so
exactly. He took up a thin tuning fork, struck it against the steel plate
of his boot heel. The tines sang with magic resonance, and he touched
the tip of the handle to the clockwork heart.

Moment of truth.

Inner workings sprung to life. Copper clicked, and the loom spun.
Budgie focused his thoughts through the crystal at his wrist and Lara
opened its beak. In the soft familiar tones of a dozen thieves, the bird
sang from its perch on his shoulder, the words spinning colored threads
of the Web around Budgie's hands. He grinned, turning to Caylyx,
signing gleefully alongside Lara's words:

"No more running away."

"We're going to make something better for ourselves."

Zira MacFarlane

Zira is a nonbinary queer biologist. They live with a small menagerie of cats, geckos, snakes, and humans. As a writer, they use horror and fantasy to explore ecological themes and stories of queer love and pain. In the wild, they can be found standing in ponds, storytelling, birdwatching, and trying to discover the latest mischief their cats have caused.

Most disabled folks have had to cope with barriers that they are told that they can get over by "just trying hard enough". We're encouraged to brute force our way to assimilation and mimicking abled people. This story is about the point after this approach has failed (burn out, exhaustion, ableism all bearing down on ability), about looking at the barrier and making your own way past it.

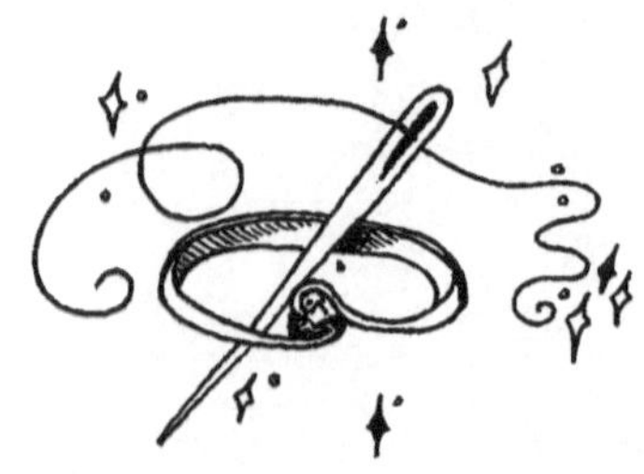

The Changeling of Brushby

— by Natalie Kelda

There once was a changeling in Brushby village. She was born in the shadow of Elverhoj, the homestead of the elven king, and the villagers always shook their heads and muttered "there's something odd about her" when she came skipping along the gravel road from the thatched farmhouse to the church.

But she didn't speak in tongues or start frothing during Sunday services. She neither shot up from her seat and escaped through the window on a broom nor did she shriek and pull away when receiving the Pastor's blessings at the end.

But she did speak to the flowers and the horses. She smiled at the hares and patted the cow's noses with the affection of a mother with her babe. There were days when she was still but five years of age where she would carry around her favourite hen in a straw basket and feed it grain by hand. Now all this by itself might not seem so odd— children have fanciful minds after all— but she would also see things, *creatures* that most certainly weren't there.

"She'll grow out of it," her father said.

At the changeling suggestions her mother would shake her head. "She's just young with an imagination. We kept a close eye on the crib. No ellwood folk have switched out their babe for ours."

For the most part, the villagers decided the girl was no harm as long as she didn't play with *their* children of course. So, she grew up playing by herself. Luckily, solitude was no problem for her.

She would stack pebbles by the creek and make creatures out of the conkers every autumn week. Then she would show her pebble cities and conker horses to the creekman while he played his silent violin, and she would host conker horse races with the gnome that lived under the cowshed.

"You are special, girl," the gnome said one day.

"My name is Tilde," she replied, knuckles on her hips like she had seen Mother do when Father walked in with muddy boots. But she quickly dropped her hands again. The fabric of her outer skirt was too smooth and uncomfortable against her skin. At least the linen under-skirt was much better.

The gnome corrected his small red hat and smoothed his grey clothes. "Nonetheless, you are smarter than the rest, for you see what is there, while they will look and pretend they don't see me at all!"

The creekman, who had been lounging on the banks while watching the conker horse race, nodded. "Never let go of that. You see the world as it is. Don't let the others make you doubt the value of yourself."

"I will never! I am me and they can't take me away from myself."

But as all adults know, life has a way of stealing. As the years went by and Tilde grew from five to eight and eventually seventeen, her imagination and confidence waned. She grew anxious of spirit and weak of health.

Each year, her father grew more impatient with her fancies and her mother sounded less confident when dismissing the changeling rumours. Because even though they drilled into her the importance of looking people in the eye when talked to and the imprudence of refusing porridge and mashed potatoes—"'cause the texture makes me want to vomit"—she still refused to conform.

There is something endearing about a five-year-old that takes everything you say literally, but according to Tilde's father, nobody found it cute in a grown woman.

"How can you expect to find a husband if you refuse to mend clothes from finely woven cloths and won't knead bread dough?" Her mother tutted, lines growing deep between her greying brows and eternally pursed mouth.

By seventeen, Tilde knew better than to reply to that. Neither of her parents understood her vehemence against marriage. They didn't even understand why she despised having to shake hands with everyone at church every Sunday.

"I'm going for a walk in the meadow." Tilde grabbed her cloak from the hanger by the door. "I'll check on the ewes too."

Father looked up from his after-dinner card game with the stable hand, Emil, who was just returned from a trip to the big city. "It's dusk in half an hour. I don't want you out there when the elvenfolk arise."

Tilde paused, hand on the cold metal door handle. She didn't dare glance back at them, but kept watch through the corner of her eye. There were two options; she could comply, which meant Mother would force her to embroider all evening, probably with the new silk thread Tilde couldn't stand touching, or she could argue.

If she argued, she would either have to prepare to bolt—and accept the wrath Father would meet her with later—or give in fast enough to avoid the regular threat of being sent away for schooling.

She thought Father couldn't afford to send her to a boarding school, but the farm had done well several years in a row. Father had even talked of getting electrics installed once the lines reached Brushby.

The final, secret alternative she didn't like to consider was to give in now and suffer the embroidery, only to sneak out later. But while Father—at least officially—only talked of the fair folk to keep Tilde indoors, she knew they truly were there, dancing round on the mounds on full moon nights.

Her friends from childhood, the gnome and creekman, had used to warn her before they stopped appearing for her. That had happened once Mother started slapping Tilde every time she spoke to them. She had taken to silence in the end, and they had slowly vanished out of her life. Still, their warnings had never left her mind.

"The elven king is fickle. He may let you dance and have fun for many nights only to decide he would prefer you never leave his kingdom again," the creekman had often said.

"Yes, and if you leave when he tells you to stay, he will set a curse on your head and body." The gnome had nodded while stroking his white beard.

So tonight, Tilde decided to argue. The thought of embroidery, or maybe worse having to wash clothes until her fingers were disgustingly wrinkled, was enough to give her courage to face Father. "You and Mother have kept me indoors all week. Tomorrow is church all day and then we start over. Surely, I can walk in the meadows for half an hour?"

Emil studied his hand of cards very closely. He was used to these disputes and knew better than to cut in.

"You are not a child anymore. You can't wander around like one." Father's grey eyes gleamed dangerously. "You are to join your mother embroidering your betrothal shawl. The sooner we have it done, the sooner we can send for your suitor."

Tilde's heart stuck in her throat. "I already said I won't marry. You can't make me."

"I can and I will. Emil went to make final arrangements this week. We have picked your fiancée and only need to somehow get *you* into a presentable state."

Tilde's breath wouldn't pull down into her lungs. She gasped for more air before she could exhale the first. The dim room spun, the flame of the candle on the table seemed to wink out. He wouldn't do that. He wouldn't marry her off to some stranger. He couldn't.

"He liked the painting of her." Emil's voice sounded as if far away. "If she can keep her mouth shut about all her oddities, I'm sure it'll be a prosperous marriage for them both."

Father nodded. "Well, yes, there's a reason I wanted someone from further afield than Brushby or our neighbouring towns. Some days even I believe in those changeling rumours, and I *know* she wasn't switched out at birth!"

Mother hooked an arm around Tilde. She alone seemed to have realised Tilde couldn't breathe. That panic had turned her into a solid statue. "It'll be alright, my love. Marriage isn't so bad as you think. You just have to stop fussing about food textures and loud noises and such."

Tilde stared at Mother. There was no purse of the lips tonight, only pity and a tinge of disappointment. Mother had wanted a perfect daughter. And she had wanted more children, but Tilde had been the only babe who lived.

She had tried. Forced herself to do things she hated for years yet it had never been good enough. "Why can't I just be me?" she whispered.

"You can, my love. But you have to be a good wife first. People will talk if you refuse to mend clothes and bake bread. They already talk when you put your hands over your ears when the kids play, or someone drops a piece of cutlery on their plate. You just have to get used to those things, then it will be easier."

But Tilde had tried and failed all her life. She felt broken, dismissed and had no energy left to even protest when Mother made her sit and start on a corner of the silk shawl. The too-smooth feel of the thread sent goosebumps up Tilde's arms and she shivered. She would rather be kidnapped by the elven king than work with this thread.

"This is very expensive fabric," Mother said. Like the fabric's price was more important than Tilde's happiness.

But she simply nodded and stayed mute the rest of the evening. Protesting or explaining herself had never helped anyway, so why would it now?

*

As the weeks passed by, Tilde was never allowed to walk in the meadows or even sit by the creek like she once had cherished. Her parents kept her under close watch, their 'schooling' taking a rougher, more frantic turn than she had been used to.

"You will eat the porridge or starve," Father said.

So Tilde starved, sneaking herself unripe strawberries and thyme leaves from the herb garden to keep her going until lunch which, thankfully, usually wasn't porridge.

"You will work on your shawl," Mother ordered in the afternoon hours. "It must be ready for midsummer and the wedding."

What Tilde dreamt of didn't matter to them. They kept promising she would like marriage, insisting she was wrong and didn't know herself best for saying she would never change her mind about it. But the more they claimed to know her best, the more she doubted herself.

Was she really a changeling? Her peers in Brushby were all excitedly talking about their own weddings. Some even paraded around with tokens from their fiancées and Lise, who had married the year before, was heavy with her first babe. That was what really sowed doubt in Tilde's mind. Seeing her friends, if those whom she had never had much at all in common with could be called friends, holding hands, hugging, and some even kissing their new husbands and fiancées.

It wasn't that Tilde didn't want companionship. It was the thought of a stranger touching her hand. Of being forced to eat things she didn't like if he demanded mashed potatoes for dinner and porridge for breakfast. Of having to wear 'fine cloths' because he was well-to-do, and it was expected.

The week before the big day, Tilde fell ill. It wasn't a sickness of the body but of the mind. She felt feverish and anguished and refused even the sweet bread Mother baked especially. Her fiancée was on the way. Father had read aloud the letter that had arrived with a courier on a fine pony.

Tilde's lungs had stopped working when Father got to the "I will arrive to receive my bride two days hence". Mother helped her to the bed in the next room—the bed Tilde soon wouldn't be sleeping in any longer.

"He's a good man. You will be happy enough once you get used to the thought." Mother petted Tilde's hair.

Tilde shook her head and Mother left her to see to the courier being fed and treated as would be befitting of a liveryman from the big city. And so, Tilde lay in her bed with the monsters of her heart roaring louder and louder. The fear grew heavy on her chest and settled in her gut.

It took until the sun had gone from the sky and dusk arrived before her heart and breath stilled enough to speak. By then, Mother was impatient when she still refused food.

"But Mother, what if I'm right that I will hate every minute of marriage?" And she was sure she would. It would be an endless life of being told what she should and shouldn't do. Of being forced to pretend she was someone entirely different.

"You will pretend to like it, then. You will behave as you are supposed to as a wife. You won't shy from touch, and you will mend the clothes you are asked to without complaint. Do you understand? And whatever you do, never talk about fairies and gnomes and the elven folk. Witch hunting may be illegal now in Denmark, but that doesn't mean he can't send you away. You don't want to be locked up, do you?"

Tilde clamped her lips shut. Father had only once threatened to send her to an asylum. That was after she spoke of feeding sugar treats to the helhorse in the graveyard when the pastor asked about what acts of kindness the congregation had performed lately. Apparently that question was rhetorical and, in any case, helhorses didn't deserve sugar treats.

Tilde retracted into herself for the next two days. She imagined a different future where she was allowed to remain unmarried. Where she lived alone by the edge of the forest and invited in all the creatures that had used to be her friends. She would feed the gnome the porridge she so hated so he could help tend the sheep and mend the creekman's rough hemp shorts in exchange for fresh fish.

But eventually Father stomped into her room. "Get out of bed. Poul will be here in mere hours, and you can't lie there like some imbecile any longer." He knew she hated that word. *Imbecile.* Some of the boys had used to call her that when she balanced pebbles in the churchyard instead of skipping around with the girls and braiding their hair.

"I will not marry Poul nor any other man, ever." She knew it was pointless. Father had never listened before and he wouldn't start now. But she had to try, for herself, for her happiness.

His eyes glinted with fury and his fingers wrapped around her elbow. Without pause, he hauled her from the bed. He ignored her scream from the pain of his grip and shook her until her head dangled back and forth.

"Please, stop." She cried, grasping around his hand to wrench herself free.

"You stop! Just act like a normal person. You wear what your mother has laid out. You curtsy and smile while looking him in the eye the right amount of time. If you as much as *think* to not eat what is served…" He left the threat hanging. The sound of his voice echoed in her head. Finally, his fingers eased, and he shoved her away. "Get dressed. Don't talk about fairies or helhorses."

Tilde cried silent tears while dressing herself in the light brown silk dress with ruffles and ribbons in white. She shivered in discomfort at the sensation of the fabric against her skin and wished she could tear it all off. Her clothes, her hair, her skin. Everything.

Mother entered and did her hair. She ignored Tilde's request to not twist it so tightly and to change the silk neck-scarf for cotton or linen. "We had this adjusted to your size especially. It wasn't cheap."

Because the price of things was always more important than Tilde's comfort. Just like other's expectations and demands outweighed her own.

A loud knocking stopped Tilde from attempting further protest. Poul stood in the farm courtyard, dashing, stiff and with high expectations.

He kissed her hand and kept hold of it all afternoon. When she tried to pull away, he smiled and held on tighter.

He sat too close during dinner. His satin weave silk jacket with its elaborate buttons, embroidery, and an even worse texture than the plain weave silk she wore, kept touching her wrist and she wanted to scream for him to stop patting her arm. Cutlery screeched on plates; silence reigned awkwardly.

The next day went the same, and the next after that until suddenly, Tilde had but one day left of what little freedom there had been. After dinner that night, Poul bid them farewell and rode with Father the mile back to Brushby Inn where he would stay until the wedding the next day.

It was midsummer's eve and fires had been lit in town to ward off the witches, and for young lovers to jump over the embers in hope of good fortune and fertility. But Tilde was stuck at home. She wasn't to see anybody but Mother, her two aunts and the five daughters they had between them.

"This time tomorrow, you will be getting ready for your first night in wedlock," Cousin Anne said. She had a dreamy expression on her face that almost made Tilde sick.

"It's the worst night of marriage, really." Her older cousin wrinkled her nose. "It gets easier after that, once it stops hurting so much."

Panic pierced Tilde's chest. Everything already hurt so much—how could it get worse? She scratched at the brown silk sleeve.

"Stop that." Mother caught her hand. "You will be a fine city wife tomorrow. City wives don't itch themselves like stray dogs."

"Fine city wife indeed." Auntie Thyra nodded. "He'll surely want many strong children for that sawmill business he kept saying he would found."

Tilde shot to her feet. "I'm sorry, I'm tired. I'll take my leave." She did her best curtsy and rushed out of the kitchen.

"It was a very good suitor you found for her, all things considered," one of the cousins said too loudly not to have planned on being heard.

Tilde tore the silk gown off when she reached her room. She pulled pins from her hair and kicked off the shoes that had pinched her toes all day. *He will want many children.* What about what she wanted? Children were loud, and Poul had already approved of Mother serving bacon and mashed potatoes the day before, which had certainly been a test for Tilde, who had feigned illness to avoid having dinner.

She dropped to her bed wearing only her undergarments. The corset hugged her body without being too tight and provided some measure of comfort. But she couldn't sleep. For a long while she tossed on the bed before rising. The knowledge that this was her last day before being forced to sleep in the bed of somebody she despised weighed too severely on her mind.

Stalking back and forth in her small room, a flicker of light caught her eye. She stopped and stared out the window, first seeing nothing. But then the light bounced past again, far out in the meadow. Who would be out there in the middle of the night on midsummer's eve? Secret lovers? Or the elven king?

Without thinking twice, Tilde drew open her window. A light quite close to the house winked and vanished again.

"Pst! Is anybody there?" she whispered, cupping her mouth, although her family were rowdy enough in the kitchen and she doubted they heard.

Nobody answered, but the light returned. She leaned out of the window when it moved, gliding slowly towards her. With a spark of green, a young woman suddenly stood before her, pale lantern in hand.

"Are you Tilde of whom we so often have heard?" The woman spoke with melody, her voice warm and kind. Her long black hair reached below her waist in cascades even Tilde was envious of.

"Who are you and how have you heard of me?" Tilde didn't dare move or breathe. There was a light coming off the woman's skin, and she knew this was one of the elven folk without ever before having spoken to them. Even the other creatures kept clear, for the elven folk were more powerful than any other beings of old.

"You can call me Morgenfrue, as I mostly walk by the light of dawn, and I am the mistress of the elven king. He has asked if you are in distress. The creekman and gnome both said so while we listened in."

Tilde could only stare, for what could you say to the mistress of the elven king?

"If you wish, you can come with me." Morgenfrue opened her palm towards Tilde, a faint smile on her lips. Her eyes were the same orange gold of the calendula flowers she was named after. "With us, you can be yourself, always."

"I don't like holding hands." Tilde looked down, her heart clenching.

"You can follow me without. We also don't force you to eat what you dislike or wear clothes that grate your skin."

Tilde glanced up quickly before averting her gaze once more. "Wh-what about marriage?" The words could barely leave her lips.

"With us, you can get married or not. It depends on your preferences. All we ask for is kindness in return."

Tilde picked at the knot in the wood of the windowsill. "And my family? If I should wish to see them again?" She wasn't sure she did. Maybe in time, if they could accept she was who she was, and that wouldn't change. It couldn't.

"That is up to you. Some families adjust, others sadly don't. That doesn't make you a bad person. It is their loss for not embracing all of you as you are. We can be your family, should you choose."

"Alright." Tilde nodded and started to climb out of the window, then she paused, doubt clouding her mind once more. "Am I really a changeling you have come to reclaim? Am I not human?"

Morgenfrue laughed and shook her head. "Not at all. You are as human as everyone else. They just can't see that. You are perfect as you are, and one day, the humans of this world will see that too. Until then, you can stay with us."

*

And that was how Tilde the changeling left Brushby and her family behind. Of course, she never was a changeling at all, but that was how the villagers explained away her disappearance, instead of admitting they had driven her off.

Meanwhile, she lived happily amongst the elven folk that continued to adopt humans like her, in need of compassion and acceptance for who they were: people with wonderful minds that saw the world under a slightly different light.

Natalie Kelda

Storytelling and inventing new worlds has been a part of Natalie's life since before she could read or write. Nowadays she mostly writes in English but you'll often discover hints of her native Danish or some of the other languages she has picked up along the way. Her stories are focused around trauma, healing, mental health, disability, grief and finding your joy and place in the world.

With the prompt being traditional fairytale/fantasy I decided to stick close to my Danish roots and set a story not far from where I grew up. I decided to set it around the turn of the century(1900) to capture some of that old-time magic as this was a time where Denmark was looking inwards and our ancient oral folklore was being collected and written down. The main character, Tilde, has many of my own autistic traits and I imagined what life might have been like, had I not been fortunate to be born 100 years later and into a family that embraces differences rather than shunning them.

To Make Her Eat

— by M. Stevenson

The fairy ring appeared behind our house last night as it does every summer, so when Lyssa's parents knock on the door to ask if we've seen her, a reluctant part of me knows exactly where she's gone.

I say our house, though the circle is technically on Lyssa's family's side of the lawn. The duplex has separate porches but a shared backyard, perhaps because it's easier to draw lines with cut wood than with raw earth. The two decks go out like railroad tracks without a destination, close enough that you can reach over and touch, and last night Lyssa and I sat on the porch railings on our respective sides as we've done every summer but the last and talked until after midnight.

Lyssa drank from a beer bottle taken from her parents' fridge, condensation slicking the glass, and I sipped a too-sweet hard lemonade. We watched fireflies glow and dart over the grass—it had always grown long, since our respective parents could never agree when to mow it or whose responsibility it was—and neither of us mentioned how they avoided the circle of deeper green and the mushrooms thronging its circumference.

"Do you ever think about going in?" Lyssa asked.

I lowered my bottle, my stomach curling. We hadn't talked about the fairy ring since our freshman year of high school. In the six years since then we'd tacitly ignored its existence, in the same way I ignored how warm maple syrup pooled in my belly when I was around Lyssa—when she stripped her t-shirt off to jump bikini-clad into the pool; when we watched movies in my parents' living room and our hands delved into the shared popcorn bowl, fingers brushing. The fairy ring and the shape of our friendship were voids we didn't touch, topics with too many hopes and consequences attached to dare acknowledge.

But Lyssa had always dared more than I ever could, plunging headfirst into places I didn't have the guts to follow. To New England for university, leaving the thick humid embrace of the south behind. To a summer internship in Boston that meant I hadn't seen her since we left for our freshman year of college, even though she'd invited me to visit. I'd wanted to go, but I was too afraid of what her invitation might mean, and of what might happen if I was wrong—or, just as terrifying, if I was right.

"Scientists say they're places a tree used to stand," I said. The lemonade label was soggy against the bottle's glass, and I picked at it, avoiding Lyssa's eyes. "The mushrooms pop up in a ring like that because they're following the shape of the trunk. It's just extra nutrients in the soil."

"You've turned into such a bio major."

"Sorry." I wasn't sure what I was apologizing for—a familiar feeling.

"I didn't mean it as a bad thing. It fits you. It's just…" Lyssa gestured with her bottle. A vague sweep of her hand, but I knew it encompassed the fairy ring. "I think about deadlines sometimes. Getting older. Like how Susan aged out of going back through the wardrobe, and I wonder… does getting older mean there are doors that are closing to you?"

Lyssa was turning twenty-one in August. My birthday followed four months after. My shoulders relaxed slightly. Nerves about aging were normal, right? I'd always been eager to grow up, rather than apprehensive, but my classmates in high school—and college, now—spoke often of their fears.

"Hey," I said, tipping my bottle towards her, "I'm excited to buy my own alcohol. Your parents don't make a habit of getting stuff that I can drink."

Lyssa smiled, but even in the darkness I could tell it didn't reach her eyes. She hopped off the porch railing.

"I'm going to grab another beer," she said. "Want me to see if there's another lemonade for you?"

She didn't have to say anything for me to know she was disappointed with my answers. But neither of us talked about it, just as we didn't talk about the kiss.

*

I'd thought that was the end of it, that the mushrooms would dissolve into slimy goo and the uncanny green of the grassy ring would fade in a few days as always. But this morning, as Lyssa's parents ask me to contact any friends she might have stayed over with and discuss whether to call the police, a feeling churns through my stomach as nauseating as accidental gluten. I dutifully text a couple friends, the ones I think Lyssa might have kept in contact with, but I know Lyssa stayed outside after I went to bed.

The fairy ring is a dark circle in my mind, a zero, a negative space where I don't dare to look.

I spend most of the day folded on my bed upstairs, spine pressed against the wall. Our houses are mirrors of each other; Lyssa's bedroom is on the other side. We used to tap out messages through the wall: knock once for no, twice for yes. We thought about learning

Morse code but lacked the attention span. Today my own focus flickers back and forth between the circle of mushrooms outside and the screen of my phone as I page between a dozen tabs on Reddit and more obscure sites that look like they haven't been updated in at least a decade.

I used to know more of the myths. When Lyssa and I first noticed the fairy ring in second grade, we were fascinated, badgering the school librarian for books on folklore. But then we hit puberty and the fairy ring slid from an interest to an embarrassment, something we would rather pretend we'd never believed in.

Or at least, that's how I'd felt. Lyssa must have held her own thoughts secret—another one of a growing number of things we'd withheld from each other in a slow starvation.

I memorize the lore as if it's one of my biology textbooks, something with answers I can get right. Iron, rowan berries, turning your clothes inside out—I make lists of all the ways to dissuade the supernatural from taking ahold of your heart and tuning its beat to otherworldly desires. I read about Rip van Winkle and Tír na nÓg, and each page I scroll through, each hour that passes where my phone doesn't light up with a text from Lyssa apologizing for worrying us, my stomach curdles a little more.

At some point, next door, police come and go. I look out the window and see Lyssa's parents talking to them—a balding man and a platinum blonde woman who looks bored.

They wait twenty-four hours before they do anything about missing adults, don't they? The mythology websites say that a day could be a year in Fairy, or a century.

By the time darkness falls, I know what I have to do, though I've never deliberately made the decision. It's something that simply settles inside of me like part of my body, as indelible as the way I've always felt about Lyssa or the autoimmune disorder that turns my own organs against me when I eat the wrong foods. As the fireflies return, I put on an old sweatshirt of Lyssa's, one she left in my bedroom the summer before college—the last summer we really talked, the summer we don't talk about. I slip the dining room salt shaker into my pocket and pick at an old t-shirt until the red thread of its seam comes loose, then wrap the filament around my wrist.

As I walk through the kitchen on my way to the back porch, my eyes catch on the bowl of ripe black cherries Mom left on the table. I hesitate, my mouth filling with the remembered taste of last year.

The folk tales say that those pulled into Fairy often forget who they are. Would the cherries make Lyssa remember? Would the memories they carry be ones she wants to keep?

I slip a pair of cherries, linked at the stem, into the hoodie's front pocket before I open the sliding door.

Then I make my way through the backyard and, before I can second guess myself, I step into the fairy ring.

*

The myths about fairies are diverse and often contradicting. But there's one thing they all have in common: in Fairy, do not eat, do not drink. What looks like a feast may instead be a bounty of worms and rot, or will make you pine for a second taste until you starve to death, or trap you in their realm forever.

I always wondered, when I read the tales as a kid, why that rule was so hard to remember—because the thing about rules is that of course someone will break them. I was seven years old when my parents explained that there were now countless things I couldn't eat. That no matter how good the cake at a friend's birthday party looked, I couldn't have even a crumb, or my body would make me sick. That I'd have to tamp down my hunger or bring my own food everywhere

I went, that I could never take a bite without checking first. I would have listened to their warning even without evidence, but accidental contaminations that left me intimately familiar with the chill of the bathroom floor tile against my shins and the turned smell of the toilet bowl ensured it was one I could never forget.

Not even in Fairy.

Finding myself here is like a transition in a dream. I don't recall what happens after I step through the ring. One moment I'm in the backyard with fireflies glowing; the next I look up and I'm at the edge of a clearing. In front of me stretches a long table, laden with a banquet so copious I expect the wood to sag below its lush weight. And thronging the table like a cluster of fireflies… my mind stutters over the sight.

Fey. Fairies. When I look at them straight on, they are beautiful, all willowy limbs and glittering golden smiles. But staring at them is like looking at an optical illusion, one that makes the mind hurt. In the corners of my eye flash wings and tails and teeth, but all in the wrong places, the wrong combinations and dimensions. My mind skitters away from looking too closely—a new thing to avoid.

I search the table, looking for Lyssa. At first, stomach sinking, I think I might be too late. But then I find her—a negative space among the overwhelming ethereal beauty, a hollow that draws not just my eyes but my entire attention. Something I don't dare talk about but can't stop circling. The only thing in this realm I can truly believe in, she sits at the head of the table with a crown of flowers on her head and a smile on her face like a tarp stretched over an empty hole. As if I'm looking at Lyssa, but only her body. Her mind is somewhere else.

"Lyssa," I say, and start towards her.

The fey move like a swarm.

In an instant I am surrounded. They press against me, tall and short and mountainous all at once, cat-faced and rat-faced, hissing and singing, too beautiful to look away from, too terrible to behold. They raise dishes towards me: silver platters laden with deep-ripe fruits, oranges and grapes and peaches that practically melt with juice.

In spite of myself, my mouth waters.

"Eat," coo the fairies. "Join with us. Eat with us. Our feast is but beginning."

A fog saturates the edges of my mind. It's only fruit. It wouldn't be much of a risk.

"One bite," coax the fey, "just one bite, to try the taste. Eat with us, feast with us. Be welcome guest with us. Just one bite, one to delight."

One bite. Just a bit isn't going to hurt. I've heard those words before—from classmates daring me to eat a crust, from servers annoyed at the hassle when, stomach knotted with guilt, I tell them I need a fresh utensil, a remade meal.

But just a bite, just a crumb, does hurt me. The words snap me back to my purpose. I reach into my hoodie's pocket and wrap my fingers around the saltshaker. The fog retreats, leaving one thing as sharply refracted as crystal: Lyssa.

"I'm not here to eat," I say. "I'm just here for her."

I move past the fairies and their tainted offerings to reach for my friend.

Or rather, I try to.

At my words, the fairies' coaxing and purring turns to grumbles, a muttering that seethes like a coming storm. My skin prickles a warning as they close ranks around me, their eyes flashing like heat lightning, their beauty turning terrible. They crowd me, jostling and hissing their displeasure, tails lashing and lips curling to show a glint of fang.

I remember something else about fairy lore: when spurned, the fey are wrathful.

I hold the saltshaker more tightly, trying to see Lyssa through the throng. Fear makes bile rise in my stomach. I don't dare use the salt against the fairies—if I anger them further, who knows what they might do? Salt and red thread suddenly seem like such a feeble defense, like sand castles against an incoming tide.

A tide that is rising with a rapid fury. Spitting insults, the fey jostle me, clawing at my legs and back, their nails snagging threads in my clothes. My head jerks as one of them yanks my hair. A pinch bruises my ribs.

And then they try to make me eat.

Crowing and hissing, they press their fruits against my mouth, hard enough that the juice drips down. I clamp my lips together as my skin turns sticky: peaches bruising against my chin, grapes bursting at the corners of my lips. An orange juices against my neck, sweet innards staining the collar of my sweatshirt—of Lyssa's sweatshirt.

But I am not tempted.

I have starved, I have endured, I have watched others eat where I cannot. I know what poison is and what it does to me. I know what it is to want what you can't have, and to turn away from sustenance not because you wish to, but because you must. And so I do, as the fey rage and shriek against me, as their tainted juices stain my skin and clothes. I think of Lyssa and I do not let a drop pass my lips.

And finally, as my arms ache from their bruising pinches and my scalp stings where they've torn at my hair, as the press of my teeth against the inside of my lips threatens to draw blood, it's over. The fairies draw back, hissing and spitting, and the way is clear.

I wade towards Lyssa as if through a rushing tide. I wipe my mouth with the sleeve of my sweatshirt, and only then do I dare to speak.

"Lyssa," I say. "Come home."

When I touch her arm, I almost recoil in shock: she's cold as brass on a winter day. Her head cocks as she looks at me, and she gives me a pleasant but vacant smile, as if I'm someone she recognizes but doesn't know.

"Eat with us," she says.

A chill sinks through me, as if I've absorbed some of the cold from her skin. But I curl my hands into fists, the tail of red thread tickling my palm.

"Come on, Lyssa," I say. "You have to come home with me."

I take her hand, but she doesn't move. She weighs more than she should, as if she's rooted to her carved wooden seat. A petal drifts from her flower crown, and she smiles again.

"You must eat," she says sweetly. "Don't be difficult."

This isn't Lyssa talking. The Lyssa I know has never shamed me or pressured me, never made me feel like a burden for what I need. The Lyssa I know skipped a concert to sit with me in the bathroom when I was sick from gluten and didn't even mention the smell or the mess, only held back my hair as I retched. The Lyssa I know has never called me difficult even when I judge and chastise myself for that same quality.

An anger grows in me, taking root like a cherry pit becoming a tree. I will not let the fey have the girl I know. I won't let the space between us we don't talk about turn into a black hole, become the gravitational center of the rest of my life.

"No," I say harshly, "*you* eat."

And before the fey can stop me, I pull the cherries—somehow unbruised—from inside my pocket and press one against Lyssa's mouth like a kiss.

*

There are two spaces Lyssa and I talk circles around: the fairy ring, and the kiss.

When Lyssa and I were growing up, people used to say we were like sisters, and from the outside I could see why it might look that way. We lived next door to one another. We had the same long blonde hair, though as we aged hers stayed light and mine deepened to a golden brown. We tried out for the same sports, even though Lyssa always made team captain and I inevitably quit a week in and did homework by the sidelines instead, while I waited for one of our parents to pick us up together when her practices ended.

But Lyssa never felt like a sister to me. And the question I've never dared to ask her, the question that could change everything, is whether she feels the same.

Three days before she left for college, we sat on her back porch with a bowl of summer cherries and got drunk off her parents' brandy. Stars shimmered overhead, and Lyssa and I shared a deck chair, our thighs touching, sticky in the August heat. And at some point, driven by a boldness borrowed by alcohol, I kissed her.

Our kiss tasted like black cherries and brandy, and the next morning, we didn't talk about it. It became a silence, a hole that threatened to open into a rift. A fear that I'd ruined everything.

A memory I'd never forget, even if I could never mention it to anyone.

I wondered at first, in the few days following, if Lyssa didn't remember, the incident glazed over by the swirl of purloined brandy. But how carefully she didn't mention it, over the rest of the summer and the two years after, made me certain that she hadn't forgotten.

And I'm hoping, now, that it meant something to her like it did to me. That it was more than a taste she shouldn't have tried, one that made her sick.

As the cherry touches Lyssa's lips, she closes her mouth, rejecting it like I did the fairies' fruit. Behind me, the fey begin to howl and shriek.

So before they can intervene, I lean in close, and I pop the second cherry into my mouth without breaking the linked stems, and I kiss Lyssa for the second time in my life.

I've wondered so many times since that night what it would feel like to do it again. Whether if I kissed her sober she would push me away—or, more like her, laugh it off or call it "practice." Perhaps this time shouldn't count as sober either, since she's drunk on fairy food and whatever this place has done to warp her mind.

But when she kisses me back, I'm certain, in the way I've always been about her, that this isn't intoxication; this is all Lyssa.

She sweeps one hand through my fruit-sticky hair and tilts her neck for better access. Her eyes close, lashes sweeping my cheeks. Her lips part—not sweet as I expected, but salty and warm. And I push the cherry in my mouth between them with my tongue and make her eat.

Afterwards, I'll never be entirely sure of how we made the journey home. Of whether we walked back through the ring holding hands, or whether the fairy realm dissolved around us, melting back into the earth like the mushrooms that encircle the ring's perimeter. But I'll always be certain of these things: the tart-sweet taste of cherries; the weave of Lyssa's fingers between mine; the sweet pulp of fruit on my neck turning to acid and then burning away, harsh enough that I'm surprised to see my throat unmarked in the mirror the next morning. The certainty that no matter what the future holds, whether I follow Lyssa to Boston or she stays here with me, I can dare to find her, to follow her, to lead her back to me. The knowledge that the empty spaces we talked circles around will fill in and mend: mushroom rings and unspoken memories and the emptiness of unsatisfied hunger all fed with a fruit that will not harm, but heal.

The following summer, instead of a ring of mushrooms and verdant grass, the backyard grows a black cherry tree.

M. Stevenson

M. Stevenson (she/her) is a writer, educator, and naturalist with degrees from Brown University (B.A., Geology-Biology) and the University of Idaho (M.Ed., Environmental Education). An avid swing dancer, she's often found dancing lindy hop or wandering the woods talking to plants and birds. She is a dual US/Irish citizen and is based in the Fingerlakes region of New York. Her debut novel Behooved will be published in May 2025

This story is a response to my experiences growing up with celiac disease, my longstanding fascination with stories of the darker side of fairy lore, and the queer undertones of Christina Rossetti's classic poem "Goblin Market."

Hope, Be It Never So Faint

— by Ashley N. Y. Sheesley

Marian's eyeballs hurt.

She squeezed them shut and leaned against the carriage window, but the rocking only made the pounding pain in her head and eyes worse. She wished the carriage would just stop for a few minutes. Just once. Maybe then she could try to settle her stomach and get the vertigo to calm down.

Just a few moments of relief. Was that too much to ask?

She pressed the heels of her hands into her eyes and groaned.

"You'll muss your makeup, Marian," her mother said, lightly tapping her folded fan against Marian's knee.

Sighing, Marian dropped her hands into her lap. Her mother's eyes softened, and her perfectly rouged lips twisted in pity.

"I'm sorry, my love. It's only a little longer to Sir Gisborne's fortress," she said, placing a jeweled hand on the same knee. She carefully avoided looking at Marian's wheelchair.

She never looked at the chair.

Even though she was the one to pay for belts to be added to the carriage to secure it and had a sliding ramp added to the carriage's underside, she did her best to not acknowledge the chair. She claimed it meant Marian was giving up since she could technically walk fine enough.

Never mind how often she'd fall or be bedridden for days when she tried to walk for more than a few minutes at a time.

Marian loved her chair. It reduced her pain, gave her more energy, and allowed her to continue improving her archery skills. But it wasn't good enough for her mother. She seemed convinced it would reduce Marian's chances of marriage. Marian wasn't particularly interested in being a wife, but her mother insisted it would provide financial security and better healthcare, and she was especially hopeful a different fiefdom would have new treatments.

Which was why Marian was being carted across the country to Sir Gisborne's fortress. He'd expressed interest in a political marriage and boasted the finest alchemists in the region. He claimed he once watched one raise the dead, another cure an outbreak of dysentery, and another expel the blood demons that came every summer near the wetlands.

Marian didn't believe the claims for a second, but she didn't have a choice.

At this point, she just wanted literally anything cold to press against her forehead, and a place to lie down for a few minutes.

Outside, one of the horses screamed, and the cart lurched to a halt, nearly knocking Marian out of her chair and into her mother's lap.

Her mother shouted in fright, but clamped a hand over Marian's mouth so she couldn't follow suit.

"Get down," she hissed and rushed to peek through the window. She pulled back the curtain just a hair and gasped.

"What is it?" Marian asked, wanting to do anything but get down. Even though getting down sounded so lovely. Maybe she wouldn't be so blasted dizzy if she did.

"Bandits," her mother answered. The shouts and sounds of fighting outside should have given that away, but Marian had just noticed them.

Now Marian got out of her chair. She climbed up on the bench beside her chair to reach into the overhead cabinet. She grabbed a long, thin wooden box as well as the quiver of arrows behind it, pulling them quickly since her vision was going spotty from standing. Her heart rate was already high from the carriage attack, but it made her breathless now.

She hastily returned to her chair, opened the case, and pulled out the gorgeous, dark chestnut brown recurve bow her father had carved for her before he succumbed to the plague several years ago. The same plague she'd been lucky to have survived, but not without permanent damage to her body.

With practiced movements, she deftly strung the bow—it was harder than it was before she'd gotten sick, but at least she could do it by herself now.

She unlatched her wheelchair from the wall, wheeled herself to the door, and peered through the window.

Men in common clothes skirmished against the guards who'd been marching alongside their carriage, several of whom lay on the ground, arrows sticking out of them.

Luckily, most of the fallen guards were still alive, judging by the way they curled around the arrows in their bodies.

Marian scanned the trees around the road, searching for the archers responsible.

There!

She found a single shadowy form, perched in the branches of a massive oak tree.

She cracked the carriage door open just wide enough to fit her arrow through. As a proper lady, she was only permitted to compete in archery competitions. Nothing else. Her father had thought that was ridiculous and had taken her hunting as a child on more than one occasion. She *did* know how to shoot at a living being.

But that had been years ago. The forest was not exactly suitable to be traversed from the seat of her wooden wheelchair.

Her pulse quickened. She could hear it in her ears, feel it in her fingertips. Before the plague, she'd been able to still her heartbeat to little more than a beat per second when she was shooting. It helped to perfect her aim.

Since then, she'd had to figure out how to shoot with her heartbeat pushing against her bow and almost imperceptibly beating against the string. She hadn't yet regained her previous accuracy, but she could at least hit a full-grown man in a tree.

Breathing slowly, she lined up her aim and loosed her arrow in the half second between heartbeats.

The arrow struck true. Yet a man's roar of pain didn't answer. Instead, a woman's creative string of curses sung as she fell from the tree, bow in hand. An arrow stuck out of her arm. She landed in a heap, her green hood falling off her head and revealing long, red hair.

Marian gasped and covered her mouth. A woman?

Rage replaced her shock. That woman had shot at her guard!

Marian flung open the door and kicked at the lever that would slide out the ramp.

"Marian, no!" her mother shouted, reaching for her chair, but she was gliding down the ramp before it even hit the ground. Relying on the slope's momentum to keep her going, she pulled back another arrow and loosed it at the woman who was trying to get up.

The woman just barely managed to dive to the side. The arrow embedded itself deeply into the trunk of the great oak.

Breathing hard, Marian pushed herself forward and skidded to a stop in front of the woman, who had only managed to climb halfway to her feet and aimed an arrow at her heart.

The woman dropped her bow and slowly raised her hands above her head.

"Call off your men," Marian growled, hoping the drawn bow was enough to make her look intimidating in spite of her wearing a formal gown and sitting in a wheelchair.

The redhead eyed the arrow only inches from her chest and nodded. She put a hand to her mouth and whistled hard.

Marian's poor head throbbed. Sounds already felt like needles in her ears. Such a loud, piercing whistle made her worry her ears would start bleeding.

The fighting stopped in an instant.

She lowered her bow and relaxed the string.

The redheaded woman followed the movement with her dark green eyes. Once convinced Marian wouldn't shoot her again, she finished climbing to her feet and bowed, though quietly hissed in pain as she moved the arm with half an arrow shaft still sticking out of it. "My lady," she said, enunciating both words more than Marian had ever heard from anyone else at court. "My name is Robin Hood, and these are my Merry Men. We are only seeking to help raise funds for the sick and the—"

"I *am* the sick," Marian snapped, the heat of anger coloring her cheeks. "What's the *matter* with you?"

Robin's lips parted. She looked Marian over for a moment. Her eyes lingered on the jeweled necklace at her throat, the ring on her finger, and—finally—her wheelchair. "My lady, I assure you—"

"So, what was the plan then? Kill us and take our belongings? What would you have done with my wheelchair?"

Robin's freckled cheeks flushed a deeper crimson than her hair. "We don't kill," she muttered.

A fire burned in Marian's stomach now. "You think all those guards are going to be okay after this? How certain are you that they won't bleed out or infection won't take them?"

The shock on Robin's face shifted to match Marian's anger. "You also shot *me!*"

"You shot first!"

Robin's knife came out of nowhere. "You are *drowning* in riches while there are women and children starving in the villages around you. I don't think you're allowed to judge me."

Marian touched the necklace around her throat. They'd had to sell off almost all their other possessions to help pay for her medical treatments and the continued upkeep of their small estate since her father's death. She and her mother had stubbornly held on to a small handful of jewelry her father had given them. It was the only jewelry they wore anymore.

Marian wanted to run over Robin's bare feet with her wheelchair. Instead, she took a deep breath, trying to ensure her voice didn't shake. "You can't tell anything about the riches a person does or doesn't have by the possessions you can see. You don't know anything about us. Or about me." She spun around in her chair and headed toward the carriage, trying to ignore the way the world kept spinning.

Her mother bustled about the guards, trying to ensure no one had been too desperately wounded. The Merry Men were already gone, and judging by the rustling in the trees behind her, so was Robin.

*

Sir Guy Gisborne—or Sir Guy as he asked to be called—was kind enough, Marian decided while leaving the dining room to find her bedroom that night. He'd seen that their injured guards were taken care of and insisted he'd pay the physicians. He'd planned ahead for her wheelchair and had a room prepared on the ground floor for her. He'd even noticed how sick she was after the bandit attack and insisted she go lie down, and that he'd have dinner sent to her when she had rested.

But he was old.

Not super old. Just… older than she imagined. She thought he was going to be about her age. Not a war veteran. Not her senior by at least fifteen years. He was closer to her mother's age than hers.

But she didn't have much of a choice. Being here was a matter of duty. She didn't have to like it.

Her rooms weren't very far from the dining room, so at least she didn't risk getting lost navigating the fortress by herself. The door was unfortunately heavy though, and she struggled to get it open without needing to leave her chair. She would have to ask for the door to be lightened or for the hinges loosened or *something* since she was going to live here for the rest of her life.

Someone had started a fire in her fireplace and the room was… Stuffy was an understatement. The suffocating heat made her dizziness unbearable.

She rushed to the window and found a door behind the curtains. Desperate for fresh air, she threw it open, letting in a welcome breath of cool night air. The firelight through the windows illuminated a small cobblestone patio lined with a short wall and rose bushes in full, fragrant bloom. A bench had been built into the wall, and she wheeled herself over to it.

Marian sighed in relief as she placed her hand against the cold stone bench to transfer from her chair. The sound that came out of her mouth as she lay down on the bench certainly wasn't ladylike, but the relief of the cold pressing against her aching muscles and pounding head was unbelievable.

She propped an arm under her head and gazed up at the millions of stars above her, tracing the constellations her father had taught her, and smiling when she found the few they'd made up together.

This wasn't so bad. She could do this. She could do this for her mother.

But nausea threatened to expel what little dinner she'd been able to eat at even the thought of wearing a wedding dress. For Sir Guy or anyone for that matter.

The snap of a dry stick from behind the wall made her shoot upright. She groaned as dark stars swarmed her vision and threatened to send her crashing back down to the bench.

She pressed a hand against her head and squinted into the yard.

A cloaked, shadowy figure crouched, frozen on the other side of the roses.

Marian opened her mouth to scream for help, but the figure stood and threw off their hood.

"What are you doing here?" Robin Hood whispered.

"*Me?* You're the one trespassing!"

She tried to push her bow behind her back better, but if she hadn't drawn attention to it, Marian would never have noticed it. "Ah, well—"

"No," she said, sounding more like she was scolding a bad dog. "You are *not* allowed to steal from or attack Sir Guy."

Robin blinked. "Oh, it's Sir *Guy*, is it?"

Marian's cheeks burned. "Sir Gisborne. Whatever."

Robin pressed a hand against her mouth. "Wait, wait, wait. Why are you here? Don't tell me you're desperate enough to marry him for the money or whatever."

She suddenly felt very defensive of the man. "He has offered to help provide me with medical care and to give my mother enough money to continue to run her estate and employ the staff!"

Robin pushed her hair back off her forehead and climbed over the wall to sit by Marian. "Is that what you want?"

"Physicians, my mother not being homeless, and at least twenty good people keeping their jobs? Of course I do."

She frowned. And then reached out and brushed her fingers against Marian's cheek. "You had a pebble stuck to your cheek."

Marian hated how flustered she felt. "Well, I was *supposed* to be alone in my private garden."

"What are you doing out here anyway?"

"I needed to lie down, but someone lit the fireplace for me and it's too hot in there. It made me feel worse."

Robin stood and walked through the open door and into Marian's room.

Marian transferred herself to her chair as quickly as possible. "I don't have anything worth stealing!" she protested.

She turned toward her, frowning. "I'm not going to steal anything from you. Or *Sir Guy*. Not anymore at least… I was going to put out the fire so you could rest in your own room."

"Oh."

"Oh indeed," she said, turning to the fireplace.

She didn't speak again until the fire was extinguished. Robin looked at Marian, who was nearly falling asleep in her chair. On her way out, she lightly touched her shoulder. "Rest, princess."

"I'm not a pr—"

But Robin was gone.

The room had cooled off significantly between the door being open and the fire being out, so Marian closed and locked the door and finally—*finally*—was able to rest.

*

Over the next few weeks, Marian was not often invited to marriage arrangements and was not particularly interested in the wedding planning that Sir Guy and her mother were constantly fretting over, so she regularly went out to her garden to read or to work on the embroidery for her wedding dress. She was still deeply uncomfortable with the idea of wearing a wedding dress, but at least the embroidery was something to do that wasn't discussing guest lists and menu items.

And at night, sometimes while she lay on the bench and watched for shooting stars, Robin would return.

At first, Marian would try to get her to leave, but soon, she found the company pleasant and the conversations easy. Robin would regale her with stories of her and the Merry Men's adventures and talked about how they all found each other and the ways they'd been able to help people.

It would have been much more delightful if Robin wasn't attacking people to get that money. But she *had* seemed to learn from attacking Marian's carriage that day. She and her crew had been much more careful at making sure they knew who their targets were and that they were undeniably hoarding wealth.

Robin once had been nobility as well. Like other young women their age, her parents had attempted to arrange a marriage for her. She wanted it even less than Marian and had fewer reasons to accept.

So, she ran away.

Not many areas were particularly ready or willing to take in a runaway noblewoman, so she had found herself stealing to survive. And when she'd found others doing the same, she formed her little merry band. She called them Merry Men, but there were people of all ages and genders who joined her too. They'd built a small village deep in the forest and lived together.

Sometimes, Robin would ask Marian to join her.

Sometimes, Marian almost said yes.

But then what would happen to her mother? What would happen to *her*? Who would see to her medical care? And her wheelchair wouldn't even make it to their village!

And her mother seemed so happy now that there was hope for Marian. How could she leave?

The night before the wedding, Marian sat with Sir Guy and her mother for dinner while they finalized plans. Too full of anxious energy, she didn't have much of an appetite and sullenly pushed her peas around her plate, wishing she were with Robin instead.

Her mother gushed about the decorations being delivered that morning and fretted about the guest list. Her emotive hands flitted about in nervous excitement—nearly smacking Sir Guy—as she repeated the plan for the hundredth time. He caught her hand, and she flushed a deep red while stuttering over an apology.

The small yet blaring movements only reminded Marian how on more than one occasion, he had invited her mother to stay and live with them so she wouldn't be alone. Her mother seemed to glow with a happiness Marian hadn't seen since before the plague. Before her father died.

He smiled and set her hand back on the table. His eyes never left her face.

Marian thought back to Robin's visit the night before. She had paced around her room, unable to sit still but always within reach of her chair in case she fell or got too dizzy.

Robin had watched on with sad eyes. "My offer still stands."

"You haven't seen how happy my mother is."

She had scoffed. "Then she should marry him if she likes him so much."

Oh.

Oh.

She had been joking. Marian knew it was a joke—had even laughed last night when she said it. But what if…?

Despite Sir Guy's repeated attempts to ease her worries and find common ground, even opening up about his past. About the war and about his continuing struggle with what soldiers called battle fatigue. But despite the kinship she found in his eyes when she had a particularly exhausting day of health, she just couldn't find the love in her heart. Not the same one she saw in front of her.

"Do you love him?" Marian burst out, interrupting her mother halfway through a sentence about some wedding nonsense.

Sir Guy blinked a few times, his attention so rapt on her mother that it took him a moment to turn to her.

"Excuse me?" Her mother seemed like she hadn't quite heard her, though his gentle eyes seemed to understand exactly what she meant.

"Do you love Sir Guy?" she asked.

Her mother set her fork down, her cheeks turning pink again. "Whatever gave you that idea?"

She looked between them. "It's okay if you do. I haven't seen you this happy in years."

"Oh, darling. I'm happy because there's hope for you!"

She shook her head. "There's hope for *you*. Mother, please. You should marry him."

Her mother looked flustered, avoiding looking at Sir Guy. "Don't be sil—"

"He *certainly* doesn't look at me the way he looks at you."

It was true even now. He was watching her mother with a warmth that didn't quite match the emotions of a formal political marriage. A longing lingered in his eyes, even though he hadn't spoken yet.

Her mother sighed. "But the wedding dr—"

"We're nearly the same size," Marian said. "Wear my dress."

"But—"

"Mother… there's more than one path to hope."

Her mother anxiously fixed her hair. "This is so sudden—"

Marian threw her hands in the air. "It's all been sudden!" She turned to Sir Gisborne. "Sir Guy, do you love my mother?"

He looked at Marian with deep gratitude. "I… I believe I do. Marian, I am sorry. I—"

"Don't be!"

His weatherworn, scarred face softened as he turned to Marian's mother. "Would you be willing to take my hand in marriage instead?"

Her mother gasped and covered her mouth with both hands, tears shining in her eyes. She nodded for several seconds before she found her voice. "Yes! Yes! I will!"

Sir Guy stood from his chair and swept her into his arms while she laughed and cried.

Marian smiled and excused herself to let the happy couple have their moment. She wheeled herself to her room and out into her garden.

As she'd hoped, Robin was already there, lounging on the bench just outside the window's light. With the way she lounged, no one would've guessed she had been nobility once.

"You look abnormally chipper tonight." Robin sat up and hesitated as she inspected Marian. "Are you… happy about the wedding?"

Grinning, Marian pulled her chair in front of Robin. "The wedding's going to happen. But… I won't be the bride."

Robin blinked. "…What?"

"You were right."

"Of course I was! Er…what about?"

"My mom loves Sir Guy. And he loves her back."

Robin fought back a grin like she didn't want to seem too excited. "You know… I've had the Merry Men working on building a path for you. It's nearly ready." She leaned closer to Marian. "One of the Merry Men studied with the king's physicians."

"Ask me one more time, Robin," Marian whispered, heart pounding against her ribs. "Ask me to run away with you."

"Lady Marian, will you join my Merry Men?" Only inches separated them now. Robin smelled like the roses in the garden. "Marian, will you run away with me?"

Marian tucked a strand of Robin's red hair behind her ear. She closed what little space remained between them and pressed her lips against Robin's. "I will."

Ashley N. Y. Sheesley

Ashley Sheesley is a disabled author and scientist. She loves all things fantasy and mostly decided to become a scientist because you can't be a wizard in real life. When she's not writing about dragons and werewolves and archery, she loves drawing, painting, knitting, crochet, and night sky photography, and was an archer before she got too sick. Her debut YA contemporary fantasy, Child of the Dragon, is due to release early 2026. She lives with her husband and small zoo of three cats, two rabbits, and a bearded dragon.

I love to include disability in fantasy settings! I knew I wanted to write a story with an archer in a wheelchair, and I thought a Maid Marian archer meet-cute with a female Robin Hood would be a fun idea— well...it's only a meet-cute if you count "you shot me?!"
"You shot at me first!" as a meet-cute (but I do).
I really wanted to write Marian with my same disabilities. Marian is supposed to have a mix of ME/CFS, POTS, orthostatic intolerance, and chronic migraine like I do even though those words are not used exactly, I tried to make her symptoms integral to the way she moves and navigates the world. She is an ambulatory wheelchair user like I am as well. Marian and Robin are both supposed to be on the aromantic and asexual spectrums, so having them both be opposed to marriage and romance in general until they'd built their relationship with each other was important to me. I'm demiromantic and demisexual so having them both be opposed to marriage and romance in general until they'd built their relationship with each other was important to me. Having Sir Gisborne also have "battle fatigue" (PTSD) was something that arose organically while creating his character, but as I have friends with PTSD, it felt important to include.

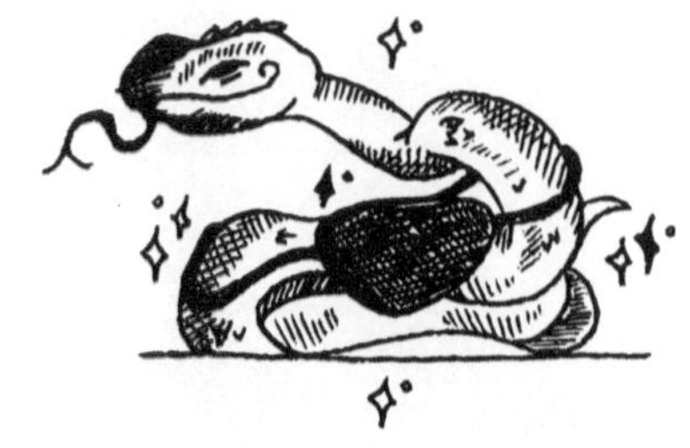

A Night For Mischief

— *by Elior Hayley*

Altair stepped out of the shadows of an out-of-the-way alcove in the palace gardens wearing a glittering, bejeweled blue cape. Gems sparkled at his throat and on his hands; he gently touched his face to check that his silver fox mask was still properly affixed there.

He tapped the silver sound-catchers that curled around his ears twice, tuning their amplification to the ambient sound in the garden. As he did so, he became aware that someone was speaking behind him, and turned around.

"—or are you some kind of infiltrator?" the woman who shared the path with him was saying. She was a full head shorter than him and resplendent in a scarlet silk dress, goldstone skin glowing in the sunset, onyx ringlets cascading artfully around her face. Her mask was cloth-of-gold and set with rubies and garnets; the right eye was concealed behind a layer of soft red velvet.

"Pardon?" said Altair after an awkwardly long silence had stretched between them. "I didn't quite catch that."

The woman sighed. "I asked if you were lost out here, or if you were some kind of infiltrator," she said. "This garden isn't part of the Grand Masquerade."

He raised an eyebrow, invisible behind his mask. "You're here too," he pointed out.

She rolled her single visible eye. "I live here," she said. "I'm pretty sure you don't. So which is it?"

Altair gave her his best sheepish smile. "I'm a little bit lost," he told her. "I'm sorry. The palace complex is bigger than I expected it to be."

"Right, sure." She didn't sound like she believed him, but she also didn't seem like she was about to call the Palace Guard, so Altair was counting that as a success for the time being. "You should get back to the party, then."

And with that, she led him towards the palace, and Altair suppressed a smug smile. It was supposed to be difficult to get into the Grand Masquerade without an invitation—which he most certainly did not have—but then again, most people who said that didn't have the means to teleport into the interior of the palace grounds, already dressed for the occasion.

"What shall I call you?" he asked as they neared the palace itself, catching up to walk by her side where he could watch her mouth move. This was a night for disguise; there was no need to ask her name.

"Dovecote," she said after a long moment. "And you?"

"Call me Art," he said easily. "It's a lovely night tonight."

Dovecote hummed a wordless agreement. Ahead of them loomed the grand ballroom, towering up into the evening sky. Great arched windows stretched far above their heads, casting multicolored sparkling light across the lawns. They were close enough to the building now that Altair's sound-catchers were picking up the music, something bright and lively.

She led him to a side entrance tucked into the shadows near the back of the ballroom. Through the doors he could hear snatches of voices already, and he knew it would be louder still inside the space; he resisted the urge to preemptively rub at his ears. His companion reached out to the handles, which glowed momentarily scarlet to his magesight, and pulled the oaken doors open.

A wall of noise crashed into his sound-catchers then spread to his ears, and he couldn't suppress a wince.

"After you," said Dovecote with a sardonic smile, gesturing to the oaken doors before them.

Altair inclined his head to her and stepped onto the polished floor of the ballroom where the king's annual Grand Masquerade was held, inlaid generously with jade and lapis lazuli. Lining the inside of his velvet jacket was a collection of components and artificer's tools for his mission tonight. He cast his gaze about, taking in the jeweled cutlery and diamond chandeliers, and began calculating what he might do to remind the courtiers that they were not the only ones in this land who commanded meaningful power.

He'd been sent here to cause mischief, after all, and the Wyrm would be most displeased if he returned to its lair with his mission unfulfilled.

*

Maia scanned the crowd as she followed Art into the ballroom, glad that everyone seemed to be in good spirits and no one seemed to be up to anything nefarious—at least not at first glance. Art himself was looking out over the scene as well, a surprisingly harsh set to his mouth, his bright silver mask gleaming against warm olive skin.

She didn't, strictly speaking, need to check. She wasn't actually on duty that night, and Sir Annemarie of Castle Black—her knight-master—had told her on no uncertain terms that she was to enjoy herself and leave the security to Sir Annemarie and the Palace Guard.

In her defense, Maia had tried to do that. But she'd gotten tired of the crowds and gone for a walk in the gardens, at which point *Art* had appeared, all blue velvet and glittering gems and a suspiciously far distance from anywhere that the Masquerade guests were supposed to be. She didn't trust him at all—well, to be fair, she didn't trust most people at first blush. She'd spent far too long helping foil the Wyrm's wily schemes to have much grace left in her heart.

"Is it your first Masquerade?" she asked Art, stepping up to his right. She defaulted to that position when she was given the option; she didn't care to have her conversation partner on her blind side.

He didn't reply, still surveying the room. He gave no indication that he'd heard her at all.

Maia frowned, and tapped his arm lightly. He startled and looked down at her with his inscrutable silver fox mask, lips turned down slightly at the corners.

"Yes?" he said.

"Is it your first Masquerade?" she asked again.

Art grimaced. "Pardon me." He delicately took her hand in one of his. With the other, he fiddled with one of the jewels glittering on his ear. A moment later he released her again.

"You aren't used to this kind of crowd, are you?" asked Maia.

He smiled ruefully. "Is it that obvious?"

She shrugged. "You seemed a bit overwhelmed. Would you like to go about the room with me? I'm not expected to be by anyone's side tonight." The Grand Masquerade was a masked event, yes, but people still frequently came as part of a couple or a group; Maia was alone tonight, and Art was pleasant enough company—besides, this way she'd be able to keep an eye on him and see if he really was up to no good.

"Why not," he said, a sudden roguish grin spreading across his face, and extended his arm to her.

Together, they swept into the chaos of the ballroom, a glittering sea of artifice and glamour from the highest nobility in the land and a select few lucky, lower-born guests. Maia was not highborn, but it turned out that there were a few perks that came with being the

apprentice and ward of the king's right-hand woman, the greatest
knight in the realm.

She never really knew how to feel about events like this.

*

With Dovecote at his side, Altair had an easier time navigating
the ballroom than he might otherwise have had. He honestly hadn't
expected to be so overwhelmed by the setting; then again, maybe he
shouldn't have been surprised. This place was full of sounds and sights
he rarely had to contend with, and up in the Wyrm's lair he hardly ever
even bothered to wear his sound-catchers in the first place. Whatever
else he thought of the Wyrm and its actions, it did not remotely care
whether he had his ears on unless it was actively trying to speak
with him, and even then it was always willing to wait for him to
activate them.

Most of the time when Altair was around this many people, he was
next to the Wyrm, sowing chaos in the kingdom. Most of the time, he
fell back into the shadows, forgotten by the battlefield.

Tonight, he had to remain a model guest until the moment *he* caused
the chaos to erupt; tonight, he was next to Dovecote, who, confident
as she clearly was in this setting, did not provide the physical bulwark
for him that the Wyrm did. At least he could parse her speech now.
He'd keyed her into his sound-catchers, so they knew to prioritize her
voice above the ambient music and the voices of the other guests when
she spoke.

They danced together three times, each set providing Altair a clearer
picture of how the ballroom was arranged and giving him new ideas
of what he might do with the materials he had. Dovecote's hands were
callused like a knight's, he learned, and the soft flowing folds of her
gown and gentle curves of her body hid silk-strong muscles beneath.
When they danced, it was she who led, even as she took the follower's
position; she was clearly much better trained in the art of courtly
dances than he was.

After the third dance, they retired to a corner, retrieving flutes of ice-cold sweetwine from a passing server as they went.

"Where did you get your costume?" Dovecote asked him. "It doesn't quite match anything the usual designers would have come up with."

He winced lightly. "Is it really so obvious?" He didn't really care what these people thought of him, exactly, but he also didn't want them to think him suspiciously odd.

She shook her head. "Not really. It's in the details—I only noticed because I've spent so much time tonight around you."

Altair forced himself to relax, smile, and take a sip of his sweetwine. "I made it myself," he said, and the pride that swelled in his voice was entirely unfeigned and unforced.

"Oh!" said Dovecote, the surprise in her tone evident even to him. "You did very well. I wouldn't have guessed."

"Thank you," he said, smile softening into something more genuine. Costuming wasn't his primary occupation, but he was an artificer, and he lived with the Wyrm; he needed to be precise with his creations, and if he wanted new clothes it was easiest to make them himself. The Wyrm tended to forget such concerns, since it was, after all, a dragon, and had no need of garments to wear.

When both of them had drained their glasses of sweetwine, Altair glanced down at Dovecote. She made no move to leave his side, and he suspected that telling her to go off and spend time with someone else would be ineffective; he'd suggested it before, but she'd ignored him and had now been with him for hours.

He was enjoying her company, he realized. Had it not been for his mission—the reason he was here in the first place—he would have been perfectly willing to spend the rest of his night with her, but he had trouble to cause, and he couldn't do that with her stuck to his side.

"I hate to be a bother," he said, tone delicate, "but you wouldn't happen to be able to direct me to the… facilities, would you?"

"I'll show you the way," said Dovecote lightly. "Wouldn't want you getting lost again."

"Of course not," he said, cursing internally.

The privies for the ballroom were two corridors away and practically glowing with magic—spells to suppress the odor, spells to vanish the waste, spells to draw the washing-up water—Altair could hardly believe the extravagance. To keep the spellwork stable, the whole area was made of ruinously expensive materials—so was his own spell-forged jewelry, but his entire arsenal could have been inlaid on these walls five times over and it still wouldn't match the actual space for the sheer amount of artifice it contained. He would never have thought to spend this kind of magic on a *privy* of all things. The mind boggled.

Dovecote, thankfully, did not actually follow him inside, though he suspected she'd be waiting outside the door for him to emerge. If so, she'd be waiting a while.

Altair made use of the facilities. Then, after checking that he was alone, he opened his jacket and pulled out several small vials of crystal ink, a fine catshair brush, and a sheaf of gold-webbed rag paper. Quickly he inked three different illusions onto three pieces of paper, added a spell for flight and subtle speed to each, and folded them into paper-wings. He threw all three through the window out of the privy, and they sped away into the night.

None of them headed towards the ballroom. They weren't the real disturbance; he had a much better plan for that. They were just a distraction, intended to draw enough of the Palace Guard away from the ballroom for him to actually be able to pull off the next part of his plan.

Altair packed away his inks and paper and brush, then took out a pair of bracelets he didn't ordinarily wear, slipping them on under the sleeves of his jacket. He dipped his finger into a vial of gold and crushed opal paste and swiped it across his forehead, under his mask.

He resisted the urge to reset his sound-catchers; he did actually need them calibrated to the volume of the ballroom, hateful as he found it.

Then, when enough time had passed that Dovecote was likely getting either annoyed with or even more suspicious of him, he put the paste away, washed its traces off his hands, straightened his jacket, and left the privy chambers for the woman who'd somehow become his companion for the evening.

*

Halfway through their fourth dance—a waltz, this time—Art drew Maia closer to his body than was strictly appropriate for the form, nestling her blind right side into his chest.

"Please step back," he murmured. "You've been wonderful company this evening—I'm very sorry. I hate to be a cad and ruin things like this."

Before she could fully process that he was now a threat to respond to, he pushed her firmly away from him; she stumbled back, just barely avoiding tripping over the hem of her dress as the floor beneath her feet began to writhe.

She turned as soon as she caught her footing and saw that it wasn't just her: all across the room, the floor rippled and heaved, the geometrical precious stone designs rising and restructuring to form a sort of dais running down the center of the ballroom. In the corner, the music came to a screeching, stumbling halt.

"Ladies and gentlemen!" Art called, striding across the newly-formed dais with his arms outstretched and a wicked grin on his face. His arms moved like a conductor's, the floor responding to him like his own personal stone symphony. "I do so hate to disrupt this evening, but I'm afraid I have a higher purpose than mere dancing tonight."

Maia sighed heavily. So much for Art having gotten *lost* earlier tonight. She hated masquerades—they made it so unnecessarily difficult to check who was supposed to be there and who wasn't. A quick glance about the room revealed that there weren't nearly as many guards present as there ought to have been; Sir Annemarie was nowhere to be seen, and the doors to the ballroom had all shut. Maia quietly slipped a hand into the pocket of her dress and closed her fingers around the hilt of her summon-sword.

"You see," Art was saying, his grand announcer's tone echoing across the room, "this is a very exclusive event—almost embarrassingly exclusive, even!—and yet, there's one person this *wonderful* kingdom forgot to invite."

He spun on his heel at the end of the dais while the crowd watched him uneasily. With a flick of his fingers, a ghostly image appeared, towering above and behind him; a gasp rippled through the room as the spectral silhouette of the Wyrm—the perpetual thorn in the kingdom's side, and Sir Annemarie's archnemesis—appeared in the palace ballroom.

"The Wyrm is *so* well-known to the king," said the Wyrm's Artificer—of course. Art. Artificer. He hadn't been subtle at all, had he? "And yet it was excluded, so I have come to give its regards to all you fine folk."

With another flick of his fingers, the spectral Wyrm rushed around the ballroom, leaving the guests ducking frantically at its passage; it was solid enough that its movement ruffled Maia's curls. Art laughed, wicked and wild and gleeful, and Maia sighed again.

She glanced around the hall—there were no others trained in sorcery here that she recognized, and no knights to be seen either.

There was nothing for it, then. Off duty or not, Maia was the sorceress-apprentice of the king's right-hand knight, and she'd fought the Wyrm and its Artificer before. It was high time she intervened.

So she reached up, moving as subtly as she could, and untied her mask, handing it to the startled nobleman next to her. She pulled her summon-sword from her pocket and stepped forwards, out of the crowd.

"Artificer!" she called, holding up the hilt. As she spoke, the sword flickered into being, a translucent glowing golden blade.

The Artificer turned around to meet her gaze.

*

"Artificer!" Dovecote called, her voice rising over the murmur of the guests. Whether that was purely due to his sound-catchers being attuned to her voice or if she was actually speaking that loudly, Altair couldn't tell.

He turned and saw her standing closer to the dais than anyone else in the crowd, holding a familiar golden sword aloft.

Her mask was gone, revealing a soft, shallow nose and wide-set eyes. The left eye was dark; the right blazed brightly in its socket, a glittering fire opal where an eye should have been.

Altair had never seen this woman in a dress before, nor had he had a good look at her face, but he knew that eye. He'd seen it before, blazing out of the shadows of a knight's helmet as she attacked him and the Wyrm. He hadn't recognized her before, but he certainly did now.

He gave her a shallow, theatrical bow. "Maia of Cape Mourning," he said. "I must admit, I did not expect to see you here."

She raised her eyebrows. "I could say the same to you, Artificer."

"Oh, please," said Altair with a laugh. "Artificer—that's so formal! You can keep calling me Art, if you want."

Maia of Cape Mourning, apprentice to Sir Annemarie of Castle Black and therefore Altair's enemy by default, narrowed her eyes at him. Then she crouched, leapt higher than a normal human could have, and alighted on his dais, her sword pointed straight at him.

"Have you a sword, Artificer? I'd hate to kill an unarmed man."

"Please," he said. "As if I'd take up a *sword*—so uncouth, don't you think?" He dodged back as she lunged, swinging her blade towards his chest.

Altair called on the magic he'd worked into his jewelry and raised his right arm to block the stroke with a faint, near-invisible shield. "Careful!" he said. "You wouldn't want to mess up my jacket, now would you? I put so much work into it!"

"Breaking into the palace is a good way to ask for your clothes to be ruined," Maia retorted dryly, flicking a stream of fire towards him off the end of her sword. "That's not really *my* fault, *Art*."

He rolled backwards, reinforcing his shields as he went, and let the flame blaze past him. Maia cut it off rather than let it burn part of the ballroom, which was as impressive as it was disappointing. It would have been terribly poetic if her defense of this place had ended up causing it harm.

Popping to his feet again, he tilted his head, considering his next move. The diamond chandeliers called to him, shimmering stones resonating with his own spell-tools.

Before Maia could get in another attack, he snapped his fingers, the gemstones decorating his rings suddenly blazing like a dozen tiny stars. The shadow-Wyrm he'd conjured took another turn about the room, this time severing the chandeliers from their chains. He caught them, gold and opal warm against his forehead, before they could fall to the ground, and drew them into a rotating circle around himself.

"You really ought to think about adding some better wards to this place," he said conversationally as Maia swore. "Honestly. It's just as well that I wasn't here to assassinate anyone—I could have been much more destructive, if I'd wanted to."

"That's not really my place," she snapped back, eyeing his orbiting chandeliers warily.

Altair shrugged. "Well, maybe suggest it to your knight-master or something, then." He knew the Wyrm would be irritated with him if it realized he was using this night of chaos for something as foolish and soft-hearted as giving *advice* to the kingdom, but—well. He couldn't help it. Maia had been nothing but undeservedly polite to him all night, even with her suspicions; he hated to repay her only in violence.

"I'll keep it in mind," said Maia, glaring at him. Her eye darted between him, the chandeliers, and the people in the room. Most of them had by now clustered against the walls—he'd sealed the doors, so they couldn't easily get out, and reinforcements would have trouble getting in.

"Good," said Altair. With a twitch of his fingers, he hurled one of the chandeliers at Maia, and their duel began in earnest.

*

When Sir Annemarie broke down the side door to the ballroom with the fewest number of people clustered near it, the Artificer seemed entirely surprised. Maia had heard the telltale signs of her knight-master's sword attacking a ward at least two minutes earlier, but she wasn't about to make the Artificer's attack *easier* for him and so had tried to avoid reacting.

"Well then," said the Artificer, his smile much more strained than it had been a moment ago. "I think it's time I took my leave." With that, he scattered the remnants of the chandeliers and a rain of stolen cutlery and jewels across the room and leapt onto the back of the spectral Wyrm. "See you around, Maia of Cape Mourning!" Then he crashed through the biggest stained-glass window—a veneration of the current king and his crowning—and escaped into the night.

Maia was far too busy conjuring a sudden shield over the guests and herself, right eye blazing hot in her face, to even attempt to pursue. Sir Annemarie couldn't fly, and neither could any of the guards she'd brought, so no real attempt could be made to stop the Artificer leaving.

Annemarie came up to her with a faint frown as Maia slowly lowered the shield over the room, gently letting the debris sink to the floor. "What happened here?" her knight-master asked.

"We had an uninvited guest," said Maia dryly. "Apparently, the Wyrm was offended that we didn't invite it to come here—or so its Artificer says, anyway."

Her knight-master hummed thoughtfully. "I see." She moved away and began barking orders to the Palace Guard.

Maia stood on the dais the Artificer had raised, staring out the shattered window into the night.

Every other interaction they'd had, he'd been nothing but the Wyrm's shadow, lurking behind it, giving his support—she had never actually had a chance to speak with him before tonight.

He hadn't been at all like she'd expected.

Elior Hayley

Elior Haley is a university student studying linguistics and
mathematics. He has been writing stories, most of them science fiction
or fantasy, since he was a small child. When not writing or studying,
he can be found drawing, painting, and practicing circus arts.

Lessons in Botany

— by Casper E. Falls

There once was a lonely soul trapped in a tower, kept safe from life and all its lethal wonders. You might have seen the light of his candle peek through the forest's thick tree tops like a jack-o'-lantern, luring wanderers into danger. Except, the only danger they'd find was a seventeen-year-old boy who was not meant for light, day or night. Who was meant to lie still in the darkness and wait for Doctor Zucker's return.

His parents had given their son—though they'd refer to him as their daughter—into the care of Doctor Zucker's isolation protocol. What else were they to do? They had a rambunctious child and his adventures were bound to kill him. When he fell ill from the soiled water of a river and the Great Weakness took hold of his young body, he'd been too restless to understand. Why lie on a bed and listen to folktales while sipping his mother's beloved rapunzel stew when it was sunny outside and Ruben, his donkey, wanted to be played with? They'd catch him sneaking out and riding his equine friend only to sob in pain and exhaustion for the next week. They'd stumble upon his passed-out body after he won an arm wrestling contest with the neighbor boy. They'd scold him, of course, but they never explained what the Great Weakness was doing to him, how it had redrawn the anatomy of man. How his day no longer counted twenty-four hours, but four, and if he stretched them, he'd lose a week. He'd get sicker like this, pretending to be normal, but they didn't believe a child would understand. It was too large a burden. They didn't want him to choose between lethal freedom and safe confinement, so they chose for him.

One day, he ran through the rapunzel fields of the local medic, laughing and singing until he collapsed. Doctor Zucker found him there, a child with too much energy for the vessel he was given. During his inevitable weeks of crashing, she convinced his parents that he needed to be kept away from everything, because everything could worsen the Great Weakness. Everything was lethal. "We must not tempt her," she said. "We must not give her the choice." So, with a heavy heart, his parents bid their child farewell.

"I… I can change," he pleaded when his father lifted him onto Zucker's caravan. "I can just lie on a cart like this and let Ruben pull me during yard work. I don't have to ride him. Please don't send me away."

"Be good," they responded, knowing full well that they meant Be healthy.

"What does that mean?" he asked. He did not get an answer. They handed over the bag of silver they'd saved to buy their healthy daughter a side saddle for that wicked donkey and promised Doctor Zucker they'd figure out how to make the next payment. Then they were gone.

Hours passed as Doctor Zucker and he journeyed through the forest. It would have been a pleasant ride, easy on the body, freeing on the mind, if fear hadn't seized his chest and dread hadn't burned his stomach. The doctor hired a lumberjack to carry him up a seemingly endless ladder. "Why the top of a tower?" he asked the Doctor.

"People could make you sicker, my dear. We have to be safe."

If that was true, he wondered, why couldn't people stop? Why did he have to hide from them?

"Thank you," he told the lumberjack when they reached the top, but the man didn't want to look at him, didn't want to think about what he'd done. Before long, the boy was alone. His room was a bleak and empty space. The walls had no color, and as much as the sun tried, it barely lit up the dark.

He, too, tried to light up the dark at first. He pretended it was all one grand adventure. An evil queen had thrown the hero into a dungeon, but brave as he was, he'd persevere. As the months passed, his fantasies crumbled and he begged Doctor Zucker during her daily food and medicine visits to let him out. When that failed, he begged her to stay. Anything to relieve the loneliness. Years passed and he stopped begging.

There were times, of course, when his body needed sensory deprivation, but even then, he missed his father's presence, his mother's stew. He missed existing not just to himself, but to others. Most of the time he was able to do little things: sing a song, count the birds flying past his window, reading one of the three children's books he'd been given. He might not have been able to ride his donkey, but if only he could pet him, if only he could feel his soft fur and stinky breath nearby. All he felt was the cold, dead stone watching him slowly join their ranks. His sole solace were the distant towers he spotted from his window. They stood in the forest, isolated like his own. He imagined a whole group of lost children, waiting for a dragon to tear down their tower and set them free.

When his eighteenth birthday approached, he decided to make a new plea. Doctor Zucker was brewing a pot of the potion that restored small amounts of his energy, when he approached. "Ehm… Doctor?"

"Lie down, Rapunzel," she said, continuing her work.

"I feel okay, and there's nothing else I'm doing today."

"Still."

He sighed and returned to bed. This wasn't the fight he needed to win. "I was wondering… after I turn eighteen… may I leave?"

She scoffed. "And be a burden on your family?"

The words sliced through him, but he'd expected as much. "I believe I could do a few hours of bookkeeping work a day, earn the copper to buy my own food."

Doctor Zucker paused. He guessed what came next—he'd still be a burden. He'd get sicker. He couldn't pay for shelter.

Instead, she turned to him with a sad smile. "Do you really want them to watch their child suffer? It would break their heart."

His chest tightened. "Oh."

"You can return when you've recovered. Just imagine how happy they'll be to have their rambunctious little daughter back."

"I… yeah…" He swallowed hard. "Actually, that… that reminds me. Could I… I mean, could we change my name?"

She frowned. "Change your name?"

His hands were trembling, but he'd already lost the first battle. He couldn't lose the second one too. "Yes, ehm, my mother named me Rapunzel after her favorite plant and… well, it's a girl's name and I don't really feel like a girl. I was hoping, maybe, I really like the brombeeren you pick for me sometimes, you know, the wild berries? So I thought, perhaps, we go with Brom?"

She smiled, a little too indulgently. "Let's talk about that when you're healthy, dear. Tired minds play tricks on us."

"But—"

"Here, your medicine." She handed him the potion and he swallowed his rage. If he got aggressive, she might withhold it, and despite everything, he needed that potion.

"Thanks," he whispered. "Doctor Zucker?"

"Yes?" She was already packing up her things.

"What if I never recover? I'd still like to live, even in small increments."

She swung the sack over her shoulder and picked up his knotted, messy mane, which filled half of the room. The tower's ladder had disappeared five years ago, the day after he'd tried to climb it for the first time. Doctor Zucker had come up with a painful, exhausting solution, the only bit of energy expenditure she allowed Brom.

"You need to comb your hair again, Rapunzel," she said and tossed it out of the window as if it were a rope and not a piece of him, painfully attached to his scalp.

"Doctor—"

"You know," she gave him one last sad smile as she climbed out the window. "Some flowers aren't meant to blossom."

The next days were full of wilting flowers. He saw them whenever he closed his eyes, which was most of the time. A searing headache sliced his useless brain to bits. Light worsened it, but the dark welcomed him all too eagerly, twisting his desperate thoughts of escape into deadly temptations. He fought them off valiantly, but when his birthday approached, he ran out of fight. Tomorrow. Tomorrow, he'd be eighteen. He was lying on his bed, ignoring the birdsong and wondering how he'd make it through the coming day with his heart intact, when the birds became louder. Their chirping turned into frivolous laughter and… chicken sounds? He listened closer.

"A chicken? Really? Your princess is a chicken because she's not climbing up a dingy old rope?"

"We would never imply such a thing, Your Highness," a second voice taunted, "we merely observe your actions and comment on them."

"Saddle geese, both of you."

Brom was about to lift his head when a sudden pressure yanked him down. He groaned as his scalp threatened to rip. Someone was climbing his hair. Someone other than Doctor Zucker.

Panic and excitement churned his stomach. What if it were a rake? No, the other girl had called her a princess. But what princess would be dallying about his part of the woods? It must have been a joke.

"Fly-bitten arse," the climber called. "This rope almost feels like hair."

"Even better place to hide the loot," a third girl responded.

Brom's heart quickened. They were scoundrels. He knew it. They'd throw him over the ledge, then dispose of his body. Doctor Zucker would never know what happened.

He couldn't sit up with his hair yanked taut, but he pulled the pillow out from under his head and readied himself. Several minutes of panting and creative cursing passed. Brom would have admired the thief's vocabulary were it not for his impending doom. Then, to both their shock, she arrived. As soon as she looked through his window and found that there was indeed a head attached to the rope, she screamed and let go. Her hands caught the window sill and she dangled off the tower. Concerned shouts came from beneath. This was Brom's moment. With his hair freed, he sat up, ignored the stars in his vision, and hit the scoundrel with his pillow.

"Ow. What? Ow—Are you trying to murder me, weird hair person?" she spat out between hits.

"I…" Brom paused. God's bones, he was, wasn't he? He hadn't thought beyond fending her off. Reluctantly, he lowered the pillow. "Are you here to… plunder?"

The thief spat out a few down feathers and scowled. "Plunder? No, we've done plenty of that already. We're looking for a place to sleep. Now, are you going to pull me up or am I ugly enough to drop?"

He looked at her for the first time. Ugly was the last word that came to mind. She had lovely brown locks, large hazel eyes, and a dimpled chin that accented her strong face.

"You're beautiful. But no, I don't have the strength, I'm afraid."

She half-growled, half-blushed as she climbed into his room, but her face softened when she saw how empty it was.

"My, what did you do? Crown a goat or something?"

"What?"

"This is a dreadful prison."

"Oh. No, it's… it's my clinic room."

She plopped onto his bed with a frown. "Explain."

So, he did. He told her how the Great Weakness took the life he once knew. How his parents, in their fervent effort to keep him safe, forgot to listen to him. How Doctor Zucker was the only companion he'd had for a decade. But he also mentioned his name, Brom, and it sounded sweet on his lips and even sweeter on hers. He spoke of donkeys and blue skies and the adventures he'd once dreamed of. A few minutes into their talk, the girl yelled to her comrades that they could relax, she'd be down soon. They were her handmaidens, and she was, in fact, a princess. Princess Fara, to be exact. She'd named herself after the heroine of her favorite storybook, then fled the palace. After she'd done some plundering, of course. Her family had also confused her for something she was not. They'd insisted she was a prince not a princess, so she became a thief instead.

Talking to Fara didn't feel like a carefully planned battle. It felt like a spontaneous donkey race or a buttered honey scone on a stormy day. He wanted so much more of her than this small room could hold. But he'd long learned that his wishes did not matter.

"You must go soon," he reluctantly told her. "Doctor Zucker will stop by for her evening visit."

Fara looked at the dull room, then at the boy who was anything but dull. "You should come with us. You can be our bookkeeper. I don't really understand money."

Brom pictured riding through the forest on a new cart, enjoying the breeze from every corner, surrounded by friendly faces. He wanted it so badly it hurt. But he could not burden strangers with his presence, so he shook his head. "I can't. Some flowers aren't meant to blossom."

Fara snorted. "Sounds like the words of a lazy gardener. Tell me, what would you need? How can we keep the Great Weakness at bay?"

He sighed. It was an impossible feat. "I'd need to lay down most of the day, find ways to avoid light and sound whenever it becomes too much and…"

"And?"

"And stay distant from people, from the sick or those who might carry whatever induced the Weakness."

"Hmm…"

"I know, it's not—"

"Shush. Let me think. I'll be back tomorrow evening, alright? If I find a solution by then, will you come with me?"

He laughed, sad yet touched by the strange girl's fervor. She'd fail, but knowing she'd tried would be a much-needed beacon of hope.

"Is that a yes?"

"Yes."

Fara grinned as she said her goodbye. All too soon, she was gone.

His birthday started brighter than most days. Hope flavored the air. Every few minutes, he searched the forest for a sign of her. The rain played tricks on him. The first glint of a cart turned into a tree crown tossed about in the storm. Brown locks dancing in the wind were rabbits hopping in and out of bushes, looking for shelter. When someone finally stepped into the meadow, he jumped off his bed. His knees buckled, but he caught himself on the window sill just as Fara had, his heart ready to jump out of his chest. The person approached the tower and—"Rapunzel, let your hair down."

It was Doctor Zucker. Crushed by disappointment, he tossed his mane out the window. She brought a birthday cake, filled with heavy cream and topped with sugar roses, the kind of meal that would inevitably put him to sleep for days—if Fara didn't show, it might be worth it. He watched as the lazy gardener unlocked her desk drawer and brewed his potion while telling him tall tales of the adulthood he might one day reach. Once he was healthy, of course. That was her prerequisite for everything.

After he'd faked enough smiles, Brom hurried her along. For once, he was eager to be alone so that maybe, just maybe, he didn't have to be anymore. She left with an irritated expression that sent a wave of dread through him. He was a fool, wasn't he? No one would come and Doctor Zucker would make him pay for his ingratitude. "I'll be back tomorrow morning," she called on her way down. It sounded like a threat.

He pulled up his hair, defeat settling in, and waited. By the time dusk arrived, the only thing calling his name was the cake. With a sigh, he cut himself a piece. He might as well drown his sorrow in flavor. But before he brought fork to mouth, the handmaiden's voice echoed from the forest. "My saints, why is this thing so heavy?"

He almost fainted when Fara responded, "Because it's a tree, you fopdoodle. Come on, just a little more."

"Not all of us had military training, Your Highness."

"Don't act like you didn't scrap with the errand boys every other day to impress the kitchen maids."

They emerged from the forest with a freshly cut tree, groaning and sweating under its weight.

"Brom," Fara called.

"Do you need my hair?" he yelled back.

"No, you odd duck. Just stand back so a branch doesn't slap you in the face."

"Or an arrow if Her Highness misses," the handmaiden added.

"Close your food hole, Berta. I won't miss." She raised her bow, a complex mechanism attached to the arrow. "Oh, and happy birthday, berry boy!" she shouted and shot. Brom scrambled backwards as the arrow flew past his window and lodged itself firmly into the roof. Hoots came from below.

"Who's the best?"

"You seem to be implying that you are, Your Highness."

"That's right!" Fara laughed. "Alright, Brom. Give me about ten minutes of backbreaking labor, then I've got you."

Brom inched toward the window and yelled, "You don't have to—" do this.

"—keep talking? Yes, yes, Berta keeps telling me too. Now stand back, you saddle goose."

Warmth spread through Brom. He was part of their jesting now. He was part of their group.

For the next twenty minutes, the princess growled and cursed until finally, a tree stood in front of the window, anchored to the roof with ropes attached to the arrow. It didn't exactly look safe, but Brom was more than happy to take the risk. Only problem: He wasn't strong enough to climb down. But Fara was already wheezing, "Give me a minute to catch my breath, oh noble prince of the tower. I'll come get you." She had thought of everything.

His heart danced in ways his body no longer could while his mind protested that the girl couldn't be real. Princesses didn't save lonely boys from towers. Why not? he countered. If this world was full of terrible things, why couldn't it be full of wonders too? After all, much of the world's sadness was the result of selfish people's decisions. But good people existed. Fara existed. He existed.

When Fara appeared at his window, she was red-faced and sweaty and panting and perfect. Excitement overcame him and he threw himself into her tired arms. She melted with enough tenderness that his brain ceased to be useful. He leaned to kiss her, but froze in the last moment, remembering that she had not given him permission. Then she did. She closed the gap and her big velvety lips ignited a bonfire for his heart to dance around.

Brom blushed as they parted. "Sorry, I… that was very forward of me."

A mischievous grin spread across her face. "Don't apologize. But perhaps, we break you out of here first so you can see girls out in the wild and don't settle for the first fustilugs who climbs your tower?"

The heat did not leave his cheeks. He let out a bashful laugh. "Sounds wise," he lied. There couldn't possibly be a more interesting girl than her, but if this escape succeeded, he'd have years to show her. Now wasn't the moment to argue. He grabbed his few possessions (the three books and his pillow), then lingered at the doctor's desk. Without his potion, he'd likely get worse. "Fara, how good are you at breaking into things?"

"Broke into here, didn't I?"

With a grin, he pointed at the drawer.

"Stand back," she said as she rolled her neck, then drew her knife. Another array of colorful curse words later, the drawer flung open, emptying its contents across the room. Hastily, Brom packed the potion ingredients and recipe. It was an exhilarating task—disobeying Doctor Zucker without dreading the consequences. Then he found the ultimate tool of rebellion. Tucked into the back of the drawer, Doctor Zucker had kept a pair of scissors. With a deep breath, he brought the blades to his hair and cut the umbilical cord to this dead mother of stone. Time for a rebirth.

"Proud of you. Now strap in, berry boy." Fara undid a few ropes around her torso and gestured him over. He forgot how to breathe when she bound the two of them together. It was a safety measure so he wouldn't fall, but he hadn't felt the embrace of another person in so long, her warm body felt like magic. It melted the loneliness from his bones.

Together, they climbed out the window and down the tree. To Brom's surprise, the height excited rather than scared him. On her back, he seemed to fly.

"Nice loot, Your Highness," Berta said when they reached the ground. Brom laughed as Fara stretched her tongue out at the handmaiden. The second one waited for them in the forest with a bag of cheesy pretzels. "Here you go, friend." She handed them to Brom. "No more starving."

"Oh, I didn't—"

Fara interrupted. "I told you he's not starving, Adelheid."

"He has never tried my baked goods. That's the same thing."

Fara shrugged. "She has a point."

So it was that Brom chewed on buttery goodness while Fara presented her invention. The three girls had remodeled their cart to make room for a bed and anything else he might need. But the true magic was the colorful glass dome they'd constructed around it. It encased the cart so nothing could touch him and no illness could worsen the Great Weakness. When he climbed in, he noticed the glass was more than colorful. It depicted scenes of heroism and saints.

"We stole it from a church that stole from the poor," Fara explained. Brom's eyes widened, but the princess waved him off. "My father made a donation to build a shelter for the disabled but the priest stuffed his own pockets. I'm letting the gold fulfill its original purpose."

Brom's head swam with questions but he settled into the cart and couldn't deny how beautiful his new home was. A world within a world. He'd be safe here. He'd be happy here. He'd actually get to live.

"And we made these," Fara continued and pulled a piece of cloth over her mouth. "It'll let us travel through cities without contracting anything that could be dangerous to you."

Brom stared at her, then wept. He'd never felt this loved.

"I told you every flower can blossom," Fara said through the glass. "But too many people want to stroll through artificial gardens that produce oh-so-important shite or are the same ole pretty to look at. And they hire gardeners like your doctor to hide the rest." Her soft expression turned into a feral grin. "Well, too bad—I'm gonna ruin their fake perfect gardens, because real nature is fragile and beautiful and wild, and if you ask me, a duck of a lot more interesting."

The next day, the girls reunited Brom with his beloved Ruben, who, matured by age, was content trotting by his best friend's side instead of chasing through fields. Brom stayed hidden in the forest when Fara bought the donkey from his parents. He wasn't ready to see them yet and neither were they. They had to bury the girl in the tower first.

For the years to come, the four of them would be known as cathedral boy and the three inventors. They traveled from town to town, supplying apothecaries with the potion Doctor Zucker had once kept secret. Families with children like Brom saw Fara's invention and called off the doctor's treatment plan. One by one, the towers of the land crumbled. The souls, trapped no longer, stepped into the sunlight and blossomed.

Casper E. Falls

Casper E. Falls is a transmasc writer/poet passionate about intersectionality, disability justice, and dreaming up a better future. His poetry collection SURVIVAL & OTHER SURPRISES (April 2025) explores chronic illness grief, unloving those who hurt us, and survival as an act of rebellion. When he isn't busy fighting the follies of a mortal body or writing worlds that make more sense than this one, fae loves buddy reading with faer wife, battling zombies as a cheese-obsessed Victorian mouse (TTRPG), and replaying Mass Effect for the millionth time. Looking for him? Just follow the trail of cats. (Or go to his website www.casperfalls.com)

As a genderqueer, neurodivergent teen eager to escape small town life, Disney's Tangled became my favorite movie. A decade after I left my metaphorical tower, Long Covid and ME/CFS locked me into a new one. I wanted to capture the isolation and abandonment so many of us homebound disabled folks experience and present an alternative. Society offers us a cruel choice: Act healthy and deny your needs or be forgotten. It doesn't have to be that way.
We deserve better than towers. I also want to dispel the myth that disabled people are difficult to love. Fara is inspired by my wife who brightens the darkest of rooms and always finds new ways to let me be an active part of this world. Not only is this kind of love possible, it should be the norm. If you feel like you're not worth the effort, remember—You're a precious flower and any gardener is lucky to have you in their life.

Stroke of Midnight, Shoes of Glass

— by Adie Hart

Cinderella wakes to the sound of birdsong. Groggy, dream-dulled, barely aware she's been asleep, she drags herself upright and winces as she stuffs her feet into too-small, too-old boots.

"I'm up, I'm up," she says, and the birds drop their chirps to a gentle chatter, nestling in on her shoulders and against her cheeks as if the softness of their wings can swaddle her against the biting pre-dawn air. They know she needs quiet in the mornings, only sing to alert her that the day is starting. If you can call it starting, when the sun is little more than a pale shiver at the edge of the sky and the sisters she loathes will still be snuggled under their covers for hours more.

Today will be worse than usual, the sisters and their mother getting ready for another of their ridiculous balls in the endless whirl of the social season. Cinderella's name will ring from eaves to cellar as they send her up and down the stairs a thousand times on minor errands of the utmost importance. Sometimes she thinks they do it on purpose, but on her better days, she thinks they just don't understand what every step costs her. It's hopeless to explain, though. She's tried, but they call her lazy, slow, worthless. They tease her about her birds, claim the pulley-chair her father installed on the stairs for her as a plaything for their tiny, hateful dogs. The birds take what burdens they can from her aching arms, but their little bodies can only carry so much.

She misses her father, her mother.

Her father was kind, took his daughter's weaknesses for strengths and taught her how to work around, how to balance perseverance with self-preservation, how to use her mind as well as her body. Her mother was gentle, a dreamer, saw Cinderella's future as a glittering thing. Taught her how to lay away strength with quiet days. How to trust herself. How to rest.

Her sisters do not understand the meaning of rest when it comes to Cinderella. *They* sleep when they want, falling into bed past midnight and out at noon, but *she* must work. She falls asleep in the hearth sometimes, because even the act of kneeling to sweep the ashes is more rest than they allow her normally.

Though today will be bad, there's a lightness underneath it, because tonight will be *wonderful*. When all three of them are gone to the ball, Cinderella will be free. She will make tea with the dregs of their teapots. She will drink it in the garden and listen to the silence. She will fall into bed before the moon comes up and she will sleep until the birds sing.

*

"No," says Cinderella, when the fairy godmother appears, and then, "No," again for good measure.

"It is your destiny," says the fairy godmother. "Your mother tasked me on her deathbed to give you this gift." She proffers the silver dress again, the shoes that glisten dangerously.

It would be a temptation to any other kind of person, but to Cinderella, the sparkling satin and the sharp icicle heels are a threat. Can she not have this one night? One night to herself, to be quiet, to simply *be*, without demands?

"Please," she says. "I want to stay here. I just want to rest."

"You *shall* go to the ball," says the fairy godmother, as sharp as the glitter she holds in her hands. And then, more softly, with something of her mother's kindness, "I promise, it will be worth it for you. I wouldn't make you do it otherwise."

Cinderella doesn't see how losing this night to a party of all things can be worth it, but she is too exhausted to argue anymore. She lets the fairy slip the dress over her pounding head and lace her up, lets her press the glass shoes onto her aching feet.

"You must leave at midnight, or the magic will break down," says the fairy godmother.

Cinderella smiles. "That won't be a problem. I doubt I'll manage to stay awake beyond ten."

"Oh no, dear!" The fairy shakes her head. "You must be there *until* midnight. The magic is very clear about that."

The words ring hollowly in Cinderella's ears. A night that late will destroy her body for days, and she knows her sisters will have no sympathy. This had better be very, very worth it.

"They took the carriage," she tries, as a last-ditch attempt. "I can't walk there, especially not in these." *Not even in my cracking, worn-out boots,* she thinks. *My legs would fail me before I made it out of the village.*

"Don't worry," says the fairy godmother. She does something complicated with her wand, and a pumpkin swells in the garden, twice, three times as big, until it sprouts wheels of vines and seats of leaves. A vegetable carriage for an unwilling debutante.

Cinderella laughs, but there's not much joy in it.

*

Cinderella tries to enjoy the ball, but she is just so *tired.* There is so much to look at and feel and take in, silk spinning on the dance floor and torches flickering on the walls and a thousand glimmers of jewels and glass and a million gusts of perfume and cake and sweat and the noise is overwhelming and Cinderella has to leave. But she can't. She has to stay till midnight.

Will the magic let her sit outside, at least? Let her rest her aching feet in an anteroom if she thinks carefully of it only as a *rest,* if she promises to come back in? She pushes through the sparkling doors at the side of the hall and into the garden and mercifully, finally, finds a bench where she can close her eyes and hear only the slightest of airs from the violin.

A pause. A beautiful pause where Cinderella feels the ache fade, slowly, as she reaches down and slides off her shoes and rubs her stockinged soles against the soft-sharp gravel. The feeling is somewhere between pleasure and pain, a distraction from the solidness of the hurt. The tiny jabs of stone remind her of bird beaks, and she pretends she is being taken care of. She often pretends that.

She doesn't even hear the footsteps, so the feet that appear in front of her are something of a shock. Smart shoes, tightly laced, polished to a glassy shine so Cinderella can see her own face, distorted, in their toes.

"That looks like heaven," says a voice, a masculine voice, from somewhere above the feet. "Mind if I join you?"

He doesn't wait for a reply before he sinks onto the bench beside her, flipping one leg up to cross the other knee with a casual energy Cinderella envies, has to look away from. He's handsome, she supposes, but more than that he is full of life, buzzing with it, animated with it. He undoes his laces easily, as if he doesn't have to think about it, and repeats the motion on his other foot until he's wiggling his socked feet in the gravel next to Cinderella's.

He sighs happily. "You had the right idea. It's lovely out here."

Cinderella knows that politeness demands a response from her, but it takes effort to lift her voice out of her comfortable silence. "You're not enjoying the ball?"

She meant only to make chit-chat, but the man surprises her by taking a moment to reply. He looks like he's really considering her question, and Cinderella is astonished by the spark it lights inside her, that he finds her simple question worth his focus.

"I don't think I am, actually," he says. "I always think I will, because I love dressing up and meeting everyone, but when it comes down to it, it gets too noisy, so I can't focus on who I'm talking to, and too busy, so my skin feels almost bruised, and too…" He grimaces, waves his hands vaguely.

"Too much?"

"Far, far too much," he agrees with some relief. "I like to come away and get some peace so I can face the rest of the evening."

"I know the feeling," says Cinderella with a half laugh. "But you don't have to stay, surely. Why not just attend while it's fun, then let yourself go home?" *I would*, she thinks. *I would have left already if not for the magic.*

"I don't think my parents would like that," he says. "They went to a lot of trouble to get me here."

Cinderella thinks of every time her sisters and stepmother have pushed past her limits, made her exchange her comfort for theirs, her health for their whims. She hears an echo of that resentment in this man's voice. "I know that feeling too," she says, and is rewarded with a smile that blinds her.

He sparkles more than her shoes, so she turns her gaze back down to her feet and tries not to think about the butterflies in her stomach, the prick of hope in her weary heart.

*

The first note of midnight rings out brassy, bellowing across the castle grounds, and Cinderella finds she doesn't want to leave.

She's been talking to this man for hours. Something about him is so charming, so enthralled by her every word and excited to know her, so full of fizz and confidence and comfort that she hasn't even thought about needing to leave, long past the time she would have grown tired with anyone else. Nothing seems too secret to say – not his hatred of crowds and queues, not her endless dreams of family, not their shared feelings of *more* and *less* and *want*. When he asks her to dance, she protests, pleads her aching back, and he simply asks if she wants to lie down on the grass and look at the stars instead.

Cinderella thinks if she stays any longer, she might fall in love with this hopeful, heartful man.

She doesn't even know his name.

Midnight calls again, its third chime. She lost the second somewhere in his eyes, but this time she tears herself away. The fairy godmother was very insistent on that point; she has to leave at midnight, or the magic will be broken. Cinderella doesn't care for magic, would throw a thousand wishes away for another minute with him, but if there's one thing she knows, it's how to force her body to follow orders she hates. She has to get out of the palace grounds.

Creaking, reluctant, heart breaking, she peels herself from the grass and shoves her feet into their glass prisons. Makes a barely audible excuse, ignores the pain in his eyes and her chest. He can't be meant for her. She would drag him down, mute that wonderful spark in him.

Cinderella takes ten steps across the gardens, hears the fourth and fifth tolls echo through her bones. The gate is so far away. She'll never make it if she has to hobble in these shoes.

She slips the hateful shoes back off and picks her way across the gravel, wincing aloud with every step. It isn't her body, this time; the bird-beak jabs are sharper now she's in a hurry.

"Wait," says the man. He catches up to her – not hard when she's only managed a few steps – and starts bending down, and she jumps back.

"I don't want you to carry me," she says hurriedly. Memories flood her mind, too many well-meaning people making her an inconvenience, a baby, an object to be moved. She couldn't bear it if this lovely man treated her like a doll.

He seems startled, straightens up. "I wasn't going to," he says, and offers her his own discarded shoes. "I was going to give you these, is all. You can't be comfortable in those."

The sixth bell sounds.

"But how will you get back home?"

"I'll manage," he smiles. "Besides, I'm not in as much of a rush as you."

The seventh chime makes the decision for her.

"Thank you," she says. She takes the shoes, slips their too-large comfort onto her feet, and impulsively, almost before she can think it, pays for them with a gentle kiss on his cheek. She leaves the glass slippers lying useless in the gravel.

The going is easier now, cushioned by his kindness. She makes it to the gate before the bells and the enchantment and the strength leave her.

The fairy godmother is there to magic her home.

*

Cinderella sleeps for three days.

She sleeps through the pokes and jibes and demands of her sisters. She sleeps through the icy water her stepmother throws on her. She sleeps through the birds defending her, raking their tiny claws through her tormentors' hair, screeching tiny war cries in her honour. She sleeps as her sisters give up under the avian onslaught, as they dust themselves off and slam her door and leave her to her so-called laziness. She sleeps as they scald themselves on the tea kettle and ruin their favourite dresses in the wash.

She sleeps through the tingling aches in her arms and the bruising pain in her legs. She sleeps until her body stops screaming.

The birds do not awaken her at the first dawn, nor the next, nor the next. They know she needs to rest.

*

When Cinderella does wake, it is to no sound at all save her own breath and the rustling of her sheets as she stretches. She cannot remember the last time she woke naturally. The last time she felt well-rested. She feels bruised, but relaxed. What is this luxury? Where is the catch?

The birds press in against her pillow, rub their feathered heads over her cheeks, and she kisses every one. "Thank you," she says. "Thank you for letting me sleep."

Her thoughts catch up with her. She will be punished, she thinks, first by her body, and then by her sisters. She wants to be bitter, to scream at the fairy godmother that her stupid party wasn't worth the aftermath, the crash.

It was, though.

Tears spring to her eyes. Her mother's gift *was* a gift after all, the gift of a moment in time with someone who accepted her, who made her feel warm and welcome, even if that moment had to be bitten out of her life with sharp teeth.

A noise interrupts her tears, then, the rumbling of a carriage crunching down the drive. Cinderella should get up and answer the door, but she stays put, a new spark of defiance in her soul. They don't know she's awake yet. Let this pause last a little longer.

A knock. A shrill greeting from her sister. The low, insistent tones of a man. It sounds like he says her name, but Cinderella is imagining that, surely.

A screech of horror from her stepmother.

Footsteps on the stairs.

A tap on the door.

Cinderella moves to get up, but a bird has already pulled the door open, and a familiar pair of socks pokes in over the threshold. *He took his shoes off at the door*, she thinks, and forgets to think anything bigger.

"Good morning," says the prince, because of course he is. How did she not see it? It's obvious now with the crown, but it should have been obvious at the ball, too. He's just… exactly who he is. He couldn't be anyone else.

"Good morning," she manages. She rubs her face; he doesn't disappear. Not a dream. "How are you here?"

"You vanished," he says.

"I had to sleep." It sounds inadequate, really, both to describe that deep restful bliss and to explain how she could have left him.

"So I had to find you." He says it simply, like one would say, *"I had to breathe."*

"Oh!" she cries, realising. "I'm sorry, you must need your shoes back." The birds have placed them tidily on her bedside table, arranged the laces into a little heart. He spots them at the same time as her; pulls the glass shoes from his bag, sets them down beside the others.

He chuckles. "No. I had to find *you.*"

"But how did you—"

"I asked around," he shrugs. "A lot, actually. I pretty much started asking as soon as you left and only just stopped now. I'm lucky Cinderella isn't that common a name." That sparkle in his eye sets her butterflies wild again.

"Nor is Aurelian," she says. "Except you didn't tell me yours."

"I didn't," he says. "I'm sorry. When people learn who I am, they pretend to care about me. I hate it. I wanted to hold onto you as you truly were." He sits on the edge of her bed. Takes her hand softly, tentatively, in his, and sweeps freckled fingers over her careworn knuckles.

"I wasn't pretending," she whispers.

"Nor was I," he whispers back. His leg is shaking up and down against the bedsheets, and she puts their joined hands on top of his knee to steady him.

When their lips meet, it's as soft as a feather, as sparkling as glass, as magical as midnight.

"Marry me," says the prince, and Cinderella's heart swells for a moment. The birds sing, the sun feels like it shines only for her. Then a thousand remembered insults, a thousand whispers of *lazy* and *worthless* and *weak* knife into her mind unbidden, and she closes her eyes, drops his hand. What will they say about her, in the court? Would having his love be enough, if they hated her?

"I can't. I would, in a heartbeat, but you don't want me as your princess," she bites out, though she doesn't know if her soul or her body hurts more to say it. "I don't have the strength."

"I've met your sisters." He smiles. "You have more strength than anyone I've ever known. You had the strength to leave the ball. To find a quiet space. To talk to a lonely prince and leave him desperate to find you again."

"No, you don't understand. I'm sure you have obligations I can't meet. You'll… you'll need to dance," she says, grasping at straws.

"So we'll do it early in the night. You can stand on my feet if you get tired," he says. "Then we'll disappear – and I'll be delightfully happy about that, by the way – and everyone will think we're wonderfully mysterious. We'll start a trend for early bedtimes and late mornings."

Oh, this sweet, ridiculous man. "I want to say yes, my love. But princesses don't need birds to help them get dressed. They don't use pulley-chairs on the stairs."

"If you do, then they do. We have chairs already, and I'll have perches installed in every room. Do you prefer oak or birch, my friends?"

The birds twitter and chirp, settling on his shoulders. They stare at her, hard, heads cocked, and she's never heard them speak more clearly. *We like this one,* they say with their beady eyes. *Keep him.*

At Cinderella's small, reluctant chuckle, he smiles gently and adds, "Princes don't usually need a manservant specifically to remind them of all the things they do every day. Or breaks to get outside every couple of hours. But I do. So we manage. We'll manage with you too."

"Don't you need someone… someone more like you? Who isn't… like me?"

"My darling, I need you and no one else. I couldn't give a damn about the rest." He swipes a tear from her cheek, replaces it with a kiss. "I would throw it all away in a heartbeat for you, but I know we can do this together. You'll balance me, and I'll balance you. Who better to rule beside me than someone who knows how hard life can be behind each person's facade? Someone who cares with their entire heart? Who better than you?"

She dares a smile. Dares to hope. The *yes* is on the tip of her tongue.

"I swear to you, Cinderella. In the palace no one will question when you sleep. What you do. How much you do. Who you are." He stills, clasps her hand to his chest. "I won't let them."

That's the sentence that makes Cinderella sure. That simple statement, and the look in his eye as fierce as her birds. It makes her heart fly, and she knows it won't come back down for as long as he keeps looking at her like that, with starlight in his eyes.

"How about this?" she says. "I'll marry you on one condition."

"Anything," he says, nodding with such intensity he shakes the bed.

"I'm never wearing those shoes again."

He offers her an arm to pull herself out of bed, then shakes his head, steps back, gives her space. She grins at him and beckons him back; holds on, hauls herself up. He is rock-steady beneath her grasp.

The glass shoes wink smugly from the bedside table, so Cinderella grabs them, offers the prince one. Without a word, beaming widely, giggling like children, they cross to the window and one – two – shatter the sparkling slippers on the garden path.

Her old, cracked, too-small boots follow, thudding satisfyingly among the cabbages Cinderella always hated to tend. She laughs as the prince gets carried away, sends the shoes she borrowed that midnight following, sailing into the carrot patch.

They leave the house in their socks and climb into the waiting, cushioned, beautifully un-pumpkinous carriage, Cinderella's birds chattering merrily in their wake.

And they live happily ever after.

Adie Hart

Adie Hart is a lover of stories and the words behind them. With a background in the history and literature of the Ancient World, and an abiding love of classic fairy tales, she writes fun queer-norm fantasy rom-coms and adventures, many of them set in her District Witch world. When she's not writing, she can usually be found reading, knitting, or trapped under her large cat!

The image of Cinderella falling asleep in the hearth is a pivotal one to the story – it's how she gets her classic nickname – but what if she wasn't just tired? I've had Chronic Fatigue Syndrome and hypermobility-related chronic pain for over 13 years, and once I started thinking about a CFS Cinderella, the pieces just kept falling into place. The beautiful heels I can't wear anymore; the parties I have to leave early, or don't go to at all; the feeling of being pulled in a hundred directions, not by stepsisters' impossible demands but by a never-diminishing to-do list. My Cinderella, like me, sometimes struggles to be kind to herself about her limitations, but it was a real delight to give her that perfect happily ever after – not one where she's magically "fixed", but one where she and the people around her accept and accommodate her needs and give her hope for a kinder future where she can simply be herself. That's true magic.

In Another World, I Twist The Knife

— by Rory G.

There is a knife in my eye.

I won't dazzle you with the bloody details, but know that there is a knife in my eye. The blade is small and triangular, with a long handle; it protrudes from my left eye socket by about five inches. Technically it's a *scalpel,* but here's something they don't teach you at those Cleric's Guild seminars: a scalpel is just a knife. We use the word *scalpel* because it sounds less dangerous, less threatening to patients, but beneath the haze of painkillers and healing potions even they know what it really is. A blade is a blade is a blade.

I don't feel any pain because the knife is not really in my eye. Or rather, the knife is lodged in an eye which belongs to a me that isn't this me, and it was put there by a me who isn't this me either. The world has gone blurry, all the colors melting and streaming together like a watercolor illumination. The senior clerics in the infirmary cell have frozen in place, as if compelled to stillness by an unseen force. Their faces, once stamped with distinct features, have slipped sideways, becoming little more than pixelated images smeared across the canvas that is reality. Even this morning's patient, the concussed schoolboy who sits before me on the examination table, has lost all

132

definition. This part always unsettles me, even though I've done it a hundred, five hundred, eight hundred times. Even though the rational part of my brain knows this visual disorientation is just a side-effect of one version of the world brushing elbows with another.

With my good eye, I look around for the Gate—and I don't have to look for very long. The thing hovers in the air near the corner of the room, its edges crackling with a light that's purple and green and blue and probably a bunch of other colors the human brain can't comprehend. Inside the Gate, a yawning darkness that eats all the noise in the room. It hums with a magic that is so old, so incomprehensible, so deeply written into the fabric of the universe that it can barely be called magic anymore.

In the breast pocket of my lab coat, there is a lighter. It's one of those cheap ones you can buy anywhere. This one is clear purple plastic, but my last was solid white with a cherry pattern. My backup is the blue one in my back pocket. I always have a backup, even though I don't smoke.

I approach the Gate, my eye still full of knife, and reach a hand in. The hem of my sleeve disappears, vanishing into the window of solid black. I can feel the code now, or the web, or the tapestry, or whatever you want to call it: those tiny filaments of probability that make up everything, orbiting each other, intersecting in every possible combination.

With my hand wrist-deep in the cosmic cauldron, as you might put it, I'm free to root around for variants that might prove useful. Nothing too far from our reality, just something that cuts out the possibility for injury. I skip over a version of events where the boy on the examination table never went out catching grasshoppers by the baseball field, in favor of a variant where the boy did go out but the stray baseball missed his head by a foot and a half. There. My hand closes around the strand of reality I need and I give it a hard *yank*—not so much with my arm, but with my mind. I feel the thread snap and, wasting no time, I plunge my other hand into the Gate and weave it into *this reality,* mine, his, *ours.* The knot tightens in my fingers, pulls taut, and the ward crisps into focus again.

When I snap back into place—when *it all* snaps back into place—the boy on the examination table is sitting up and rubbing his head in wonder. The nasty bruise just above his right temple has vanished, along with all other symptoms of the concussion. The scalpel sits in a little tray with the other surgical tools, clean and unused, but the knife that no one else can see remains lodged in my cornea. All around me, the room has gone back to the way it was, the weave of our reality settling back into place around the new strand. My colleagues flit about in scrubs, filling out paperwork and running tests. Another cleric fastens a blood pressure cuff around the boy's upper arm and hands him a lollipop. The Gate, crackling with energy a moment ago, is nowhere to be seen.

While the Head Cleric speaks with the patient's family, I strip my gloves off and turn to the little placard mirror that hangs above the sink. My eye is fine, I know, but I need to get the phantom knife out soon. I can see it hovering there, transparent and insubstantial, evidence of a reality dipped-into but ultimately left behind.

When I'm safe to do so, I slip into the staff bathroom and take out my lighter. I flick the wheel three, four times, and watch for the little burst of flame. When I've watched the flame bob lazily for about a minute, I replace the lighter in my pocket and turn to the bathroom mirror. White sclera, brown iris, dark pupil. No scalpel in sight, and certainly no trace of a wound.

Later, in the mess hall, one of the paramedics slaps me on the back.

"That was one hell of a Splice," he says, running a hand through his crew-cut. I can tell he hasn't been with the Guild for very long by the ruddy excitement on his face; this guy has never seen a Splicer work before. I'm his first.

"You saw that?" My voice is kind of hoarse, but I pitch it up so I sound nice and approachable and not like I do scary magic that freaks everyone out.

"Yeah, I was the guy, uh. The guy with the clipboard. In the back." The medic gives me an easygoing, apologetic smile. "Been on staff for a week but they didn't let me into the Splicing ward 'til now," he says by way of introduction. "My supervisor wants me to do more observations, so we might be seeing each other around."

"Yeah." I try to smile, but I am already so tired. "Maybe."

We're in the lunch line, but all I want is a coffee. I think about leaving to grab some other caffeinated beverage from the vending machine in the hall outside. I take a step away from the queue but the intern medic steps with me, blocking my path to the door.

"Listen, is it okay if I pick your brain?" He looks nervous, but more than anything he looks eager. His hairline is starting to look sweaty. "About Splicing, I mean. I'm doing my thesis on how the Guild is incorporating magic into modern medicine."

I want to tell him no and I'm about to do just that, when I realize that if he doesn't hear about this from me, he will hear about it on a news broadcast or on one of those late-night talk shows or from a wacko nutjob on the internet who thinks people like me ought to be locked up. I check my watch, but it's mostly for show.

"I'm due back at the ward in 20 minutes. Will that be enough time?"

*

It's estimated that one in forty people will develop obsessive-compulsive disorder over the course of their lives. That may sound like a lot, but it's only two percent of the population, and of those people an even smaller percentage will develop the form of OCD that makes

Splicing possible. Which makes the work we do rare and vital and, if you contract with a private hospital instead of a guild, expensive.

"I thought magical thinking was pretty normal," says the intern medic whose name I've learned is Euan, leaning too far forward in his seat. "I mean, isn't that what religion is?"

We've found a quiet corner of the dining hall, under a massive stone arch embossed with a runic inscription that wore away long ago. Carved into the archway above, an imposing relief statue depicting the Lady of Blight looms over us. My coffee is growing cold where it sits between us on the table.

I frown, trying to convey my distaste as politely as I can. "Not if you're religious."

"Are you?"

"Am I what?"

"Religious."

"Not anymore."

Euan spreads his hands as if he's shown me something. Like he's conducting an indivisible PowerPoint presentation. "See?"

"It doesn't work that way." I shake my head. "Religious OCD is a thing, yeah, but plenty of religious people are perfectly healthy. Same for people with superstitions." I wrack my brain for examples. "Four-leaf-clover, lucky rabbit's foot, whatever. Right. But for people with OCD, magical thinking is much more disruptive."

Euan looks puzzled. My eyes keep darting to the sigils inked around his wrists. They're in a different script than mine, and where my throat is encircled by a ring of runes, his is absent of markings.

"I call them cutscenes," I hear myself tell him as my brain screams at me to shut up. "Like. Y'know. Like in a video game? But the term you're probably more familiar with is intrusive thoughts."

I've never liked that phrase, because what happens to me is more than a fleeting thought. It's immersive. I see a knife and become convinced I will drive it into my eye. I see an oncoming car and become convinced I will step in its path. I see a cliff and become convinced I will simply walk straight off the edge.

Euan's still got that look of confusion plastered across his face, so I grasp at the only concrete example within reach.

"You were there," I tell him, "earlier, in the triage ward. What did that procedure look like to you?"

Euan shrugs, leaning back to sip at the contents of his own mug. "One moment, that kid's head was busted. Next thing you know, he's back in one piece again."

"What about me?" I ask intently. I'm looking him in the eye now, but he doesn't shy away. "What did you see me do?"

A little crease forms between Euan's brows. "Nothing. I mean, you. You didn't move." He hesitates. "Right? That's why I was, y'know. Impressed."

"What I did," I tell him, "was look at the scalpel. With the tools, the ones in the operating tray. That's how a Splice begins."

I pull three sugar packets from the pocket of my scrubs and rip the top of one open. Euan watches with an expression of polite judgment as I sprinkle the sugar across the surface of the table in a line. I could crack a joke about how, if any of the senior clerics came by, they'd think we're doing cocaine on the clock—but I keep that one to myself.

"This," I tell him, gesturing to the stripe of granulated sugar before us, "is our universe. Following?"

Euan nods for me to go on. I rip the second packet open and empty it onto the table into a neat little pile a few inches away from the line.

"And this is everything else."

"Everything else?"

"All the other universes."

I crumple up the two empty sugar packets and stuff them in my pocket. Now I hold up the third sugar packet, the one that's still intact. "And *this* is an intrusive thought."

I bring the stiff edge of the packet down until it hits the surface of the table, biting the trail of sugar in two. Then I lift the packet again, use its edge to scoop up a little bit of the sugar from the everything pile. My movements are slow and exaggerated, to make this easier for Euan. I watch his eyes as they track the packet's journey through empty air. Carefully, so carefully, I transfer the sugar from the packet to the table's surface, using it to fill in the little break in the line.

"Splicers use those intrusive thoughts to trigger a break in reality, so that we can weave in bits of other realities." I straighten up. "Make sense now?"

Euan regards the little diorama I've laid out for him, coffee cup forgotten. Eventually, rubs a hand over his face. "Sorry, I'm getting lost. I just don't see how—" He pauses, then begins again. "People get intrusive thoughts all the time, though, don't they?"

I take a deep breath. My frustration has melted away somehow, leaving behind only a strange kind of fathomless dedication. I'm not sure why, but suddenly I want to make this man understand. He asked, right? He asked for this. I never asked for this, but he did.

"Above all," I tell him, and I lean in close now, my careless arm making an apocalyptic wasteland of the little sugar universes I'd so gently planned just minutes earlier. "Above all, OCD is a cycle perpetuated by a corrupted causality. OCD is a cause-and-effect relationship where the cause and the effect have no relation to one another under the proper laws of physics. They're only related in the mind of the Splicer."

When I was a kid, I'd been sure I was going to kill my family: mother, father, baby sister, all of them. I didn't know how they would die (house fire, food poisoning, car crash, gas leak) but I knew what I had to do to stop it. I would look at a clock, and if the clock was close to the top of the hour—let's say, 6:58 PM—I would suck in as much air as I could and hold it in my lungs until the clock ticked its way to 7 PM. If I did not do this, it would kill everyone I had ever cared about. My nine-year-old brain didn't know what "it" was, only that *something* would kill them, and that it all depended on my ability to hold my breath. Some part of me knew this was incorrect, maybe even insane, but I couldn't risk it. I did this again and again over the next two years, until it became too difficult to hide. When I told my mother about my ritual, she threw away every clock in the house and sent me to therapy, where a middle-aged woman with thin lips told me in no uncertain terms that I had been very, very lucky thus far.

Have you ever seen something that upset you? She'd asked me. *A vision of something bad happening?*

I saw them every time I looked at a clock. My mother drowning in the river. My father's truck exploding into a million pieces, erupting into flame on the highway.

What you're experiencing, the psychiatrist told me, *is called an obsessive-compulsive cycle. The clock, and the danger you feel it presents to your family, is the obsession. Holding your breath is the compulsion. You perform the compulsion in order to temporarily neutralize the obsession. Do you understand?*

I remember nodding. I had understood that conversation better than I had understood any other in my whole life. I remember asking the therapist what would happen to me. At the time I'd been afraid that my condition marked me with some sort of inexplicable deviance, that black-robed guards would come to haul me away to a dungeon any moment. The psychiatrist gave me only a hard look.

You will either get better, she had said, *or you will get worse. Performing your compulsions may help you feel better in the short-term. But the more you perform them, the stronger the connection between the obsession and compulsion becomes. You will spend hours performing your compulsions, until they become so central to your lifestyle that you can no longer function in society.*

I still recall how the leather seat of her couch stuck to the backs of my legs.

Or, my psychiatrist went on, looking very severe, *you can choose to get better. Your progress will depend upon a strict regimen of what we call exposure and response prevention. That means you will be prompted to repeatedly trigger your obsessions, so you can learn to resist your compulsions. Does that sound like something you can do?*

I don't remember what I told her then. Perhaps I said nothing, and let my silence do the talking for me. What I do know is that her next remark would change the course of my life forever.

There is, said the psychiatrist with grudging reluctance, *a third option, which involves prolonging your condition but managing the symptoms. You will need parental consent, of course—there's a horrendous amount of paperwork involved. But patients report that the work can be… gratifying.*

I swung my feet while she fished a thick stack of forms out of a drawer. I think the drawer had been green. I think that office had a painting hanging above the desk. In my memory, which I have learned not to trust, the painting depicts the Lady of Blight vanquishing the Sun. Her heavenly javelin pierces the red orb and its blood rushes out to cover the land as the psychiatrist sits up and asks me, *Have you ever heard of a kind of sorcery known as Splicing?*

My lighter sits in my breast pocket, right next to my heart.

"When most people have intrusive thoughts," I tell Euan, "they can just ignore them. But if you've got OCD, it's… different. More intense. The thought unfolds into a scene, like a vision of what would happen if you do the thing your brain is telling you to do, and you can't skip it. It's unskippable—"

"Right. Cutscene." Euan is looking at me with understanding now. "Okay."

"—*Unless* you perform your compulsion," I continue, "which basically lets your brain force-quit the scene. For most people like me, treatment demands that they stop doing these rituals, which is really hard. It makes you feel unsafe for a little while, but ultimately it's supposed to be good for you. If you can break that connection between obsession and compulsion, you've basically cured yourself."

Euan's jaw works, like he's struggling to chew something sinewy, a piece of gristle his teeth can't quite grind up. His drink is stone cold now. He does not blink.

"But you don't want to be cured," he says at last. He glances down at the burns covering my fingers, then glances away again. He's been very kind so far about not saying anything.

"I'm a Splicer." My smile is a knife, it must be. It feels sharp in my face, jagged, like I've got a mouthful of glass. "If I was cured, I'd be out of a job."

*

After my shift ends, I visit my grandmother's grave.

It's a narrow slab of granite, crusted over with lichen now, running through a solid metal disc of burnished iron—the same stylized representation of the lance-skewered Sun that hangs above every altar in every temple in the land. The stone grave marker only comes up to my torso when I'm standing, and that feels wrong, so I kneel on the grass so I can slip into its shadow. Next to her, I am small. That's how it always was when she was alive, and that's how it ought to be now.

The light is failing and the bugs are starting to come out. A vine of morning glories snakes over the nearby tombs, which are not well-kept by the descendants of their dead, and I take a moment to sit and judge them, these people I don't know who are too busy to clear away the overgrowth.

I was ten when I'd told my grandmother my secret: that if I didn't hold my breath, she would die just like my mother and father and sister would die. My grandmother nodded like she'd heard this story before, and her reaction so surprised me that for a moment I'd wondered whether I really had already told her and forgotten about it.

"Oh, I don't plan to kick the bucket any time soon," she'd chuckled in that old person way that used to unsettle me. "I'll be here 'til I'm one-hundred-and-three. That's how long *my gran* lived, and I can't let that old bat show me up, Lady guide her soul."

We were on the back porch drinking cold barley tea. Inside, I could hear my parents arguing over the electric bill.

"But what if I make you?" I'd asked insistently. She was shucking soybean pods from her wicker chair, and I stooped down to peer into the bucket.

My grandmother had laughed. "You think you have that kind of power over me, child?"

I'd nodded then. I did think that. I had power over everything. Can you imagine anything so frightening as that? My grandmother quit her shucking and bent her body close to mine, even though it must have hurt her back.

"Let me tell you something, hm? A secret for a secret."

"When I was your age, I had these fears too. I still have them. I used to hold my breath like you do, or jump seven times on the spot, or make the sign of the Sun until my arms went sore."

No one had ever told me there were people like me, that my thoughts were not some blasphemous anomaly but a part of a vast and intricate pattern that could, in its infinite wisdom and infinite cruelty, include someone as strong and fair as my grandmother.

"I'll tell you what," she'd said, her large calloused hands coming down like the veil of night to envelop my small ones. "How about you take this, hm?"

Something cold and metallic pressed into my palms, and when she pulled back I found my fingers clasped around a small silver lighter that I'd seen her sometimes carry on a chain around her neck, under her blouse, though I'd never seen her smoke cigars or burn incense.

"One day," she told me patiently, "I decided that jumping-jacks and holding my breath were taking up too much of myself. So I went to the market and bought the prettiest lighter I could find, and I made up my mind right there and then—that whenever those fears started creeping up on me, I'd just turn the light on."

I don't think I'd said anything then, not even *thank you*. A thank you was too flimsy a payment for the thing I had felt in that moment.

"Remember," she'd said, going back to her work. "You don't always have to give up the things that help you. There are people, I expect, who'll want to fix you when you're older. But if their way of fixing you is to twist you into some shape that hurts, you might be better off without their charity. You can find your own way. You remember that."

This grave is empty. There's a fun fact for you.

I was eleven when my grandmother died. There was no body, and the official police report categorized her as a missing person, presumed dead. But I knew she was gone from this world and had no intention of coming back.

I still see her sometimes, when I'm working, when a Gateway opens into another reality and my hands are stuck in the guts of time and space and probability, and for a fraction of a second I can see her gnarled face staring back at me out of the blackness. And I know that when she suspected her time was coming, she merely opened a rift in the fabric of this world and slipped right out, and into somewhere else.

Rory G.

Rory G. is an essayist, educator, and horror writer currently based in Texas, where they teach medieval literature for a living. Their short fiction has featured in British Fantasy Award-nominated anthology series "The Book of Queer Saints" (Medusa Haus 2023) and will feature in the forthcoming "Little Guts," a gore anthology from Little Ghosts press. Their nonfiction has featured in the Austin-American Statesman and Apocalypse Confidential. You can find Rory online @ gilhouligan on all platforms.

The Knife That Makes The Cut

— *by Lynne Sargent*

Three roads converged on the banks of a red lake whose shores had seen many tears, no small number of them belonging to Typhania, the watcher. She watched as three travelers approached, each upon their own road, and yet, understanding the magic of this place, she knew it might as well have been the same. She did not yet know the travelers or their stories—there were so many roads that led here after all—but what was certain was that each nursed their own pains.

First came a middle-aged veteran, Alaric. He kept his arm in a sling, and hunched over it as protectively as a rabid dog, stumbling down his road. He had found his way here two years after he came home from the war. Every day since his arm had ached, and every day he longed for the bottle to block out the suspicion that perhaps his pain was punishment for all those he had slain. His wife cast him out when it became clear the bottle would not cure his pain, but ejecting him would end hers and all the anger she had borne since his return. He pleaded that he could be better, that he would not hurt her anymore, but she would not suffer him again. Alone in the streets, kept warm only by the fires of his indignation, he had remembered the whispers of his comrades in the medical tent, about mystical waters that would cure any ills. So, he had set out to find the red lake at the crossroads and prove his wife wrong, to win all the joys of life back just like they had won the war.

Second came a skeletal young woman, Eudia. She almost blew in the wind, her stomach concave and taut as a sail, her face twisted in a grimace. She had found her way here via a bad gamble, after beginning life as a waitress at the kind of establishment frequented by gentlemen with more money than sense. Seeing the sparkle in their eyes and their pockets, she soon found herself on the other side of the bar, playing for their riches and their hearts. She did not quite remember the exact sequence of invitations that landed her in the Eleronian underworld, playing high stakes roulette with poison, but she remembered how the loss burned both her organs and her pride. The witch who saved her for a substantial portion of her fortune said she would not die so long as she could make herself eat, and if she couldn't there were the waters at the end of the world. After months of wasting away, each spoonful of gruel a stab in the gut, Eudia set out on the road, determined to satiate all her hungers once again.

Last came an elder, Ivalon. They took halting steps along their road, looking more hurt than human, more wound than flesh. All they could remember was pain: the coming of their moontides, the beatings of their father, and the pain like stinging bees that took up residence in their bones without rhyme or reason. Yet what they could not suffer was the pain caused by the loss of their husband, Helo, some few months past. It was a pain greater than any they could have imagined, and their imagination for such things was vast indeed. Their dearest and oldest friend, a chirurgeon named Boram, bid them seek the old paths lest they die of a broken heart. Boram knew as well as anyone what Ivalon had lived through, and was one of the few besides Helo who had never intimated that Ivalon exaggerated their pain. It was for Boram's sake more than for their own that Ivalon set upon the path.

Boram had tried to cure them for many years, and the journey he spoke of to prove themself worthy of the waters had never seemed worth it, not when they had a life with Helo. But now there was nothing, and they might as well give charity to the theories of a dear friend before they finally succumbed.

All converged on the banks of this place that was, to Typhania the watcher's knowledge, some part of hell brought forth into reality by a vengeful god, made to beckon and release those who already lived entrapped in eternal torture. Roads from everywhere led here, so long as the one who walked the road was already acquainted with some flavor of hell. Typhania gripped her cane tightly, remembering how she herself had come to this place, how embittered she had been after her leg was shattered.

She had been lucky in the travelers she found when she first came here, that she and another, Lilie, had broken the curse and that the watcher of Typhania's days had been able to bring them home. Now, Typhania was the watcher, and her duty was to the living. Today she hoped to save these travelers the way she had been saved—if only they too could break the curse. Only then would the magic of this place allow her to venture from the shadow of the trees and the reeds and onto the boat's beach to speak to them.

Some foolhardy sorcerer, following in the footsteps of some god's twisted idea of mercy, had made the boat that rested on the bank of the lake. It made the end of the travelers' journey swift and easy, for he could think of no better solution for those who found themselves upon this road in the first place. The boat would bring these travelers, as it had brought so many others, to their ill-fated doom, and all Typhania could do was wait, and hope.

*

The three travellers arrive at the boat sharing an understanding. Each has come for the same reason, to find the magical waters said to feed this rust-red lake, to find at its far shores a curative waterfall coming from the heavens itself.

Ivalon is first to speak. "Might we all go together and share the rowing duties?" If Helo were here he would have rowed them all, but he is not. Still, Ivalon will do what they are able before the end.

Alaric looks them up and down, and dismisses them quickly, seeing only their age and feebleness. "Journeys such as this are meant to be taken alone. I have spent enough time bearing the weight of others."

Eudia naïvely looks from man to elder. "Who shall go first then?"

But Alaric is already entering the boat, lashing the oar to the stump of his wrist.

Ivalon places their hand on the young woman's arm. "It's okay. We can wait."

Typhania watches, knowing how it will go. How Alaric's hands will blister long before he arrives at the waterfall. How he will fatigue, and thirst, and then upon seeing the silver streams pouring down from the heavens, how he will whoop with joy and jump into the waters, sure that the silver will stave off that boiling rust-red, that its magic will save him. How the waters will take him nonetheless, filling his nostrils and the space behind his eyelids and every pore besides, just as his pain and rage has done ever since the war. How, finally, he will succumb, perhaps as he always wished.

Eudia and Ivalon set up camp for the night. Eudia lusts after Ivalon's well-packed meal, only able to eat broth herself. Ivalon tries to plant the seed that even though Alaric went alone, it does not mean Eudia must. They've tried to demonstrate that they are not greedy, and offered the next spot to Eudia. They have endured their suffering so long, what they feel now in the wake of Helo's death is but a new flavor of pain. They can last another day.

The next morning the boat has returned, as empty and gleaming as it was when they first met, as it was when Typhania first came to these shores.

"You will slow me down, elder. I'm sorry, but I am desperate, unable to satiate my hunger, each bite a knife in my gut. Perhaps you do not remember living unencumbered but…"

"You're right. I don't remember. But I do know that a terrible burden is lightened when it's shared."

"If only the weight of persons were the same."

The girl's words cut deep, reminding Ivalon of every time they have been branded a burden. They murmur, "I hope you don't believe in the words of those who have called you burden, child."

But Eudia has already turned away, and begun to row.

Typhania walks along the bank, following Eudia's boat for a little while, though her bones ache and her cane sticks in the mud. At least this way Eudia will not be alone for so much of the end, even if she doesn't know it.

As Eudia settles into the rhythm of rowing, it is as if the waters themselves speed her along. She sweats. Her heart palpitates like it used to at the gambling table, like it did the night she made her foolish bet over the poison. She approaches the silver falls too fast, recklessly pushing beyond her capabilities. She cannot stop it, and dashes herself on the rocks at the waterfall's base, her bones splintering alongside the boat, both of their shattered bodies left to be pummeled by the torrent.

Typhania can do nothing for the girl, just as she could do nothing for Alaric, but Ivalon… In the morning she will be able to speak with them, the curse of silence that prevents her from revealing the truth of this place to the travelers temporarily broken, for they have asked for help and offered it. When it is their turn, she will be there. She will do what she can, what she comes here to do.

Ivalon spends a long day and night waiting for the boat to return. They wonder about all the stories they have heard in their long years, how many times they have been encouraged to go down this bloodstained road. But if all the wisewomen, and witches, and chirurgeons have not had the answer to their pains, why, really, should they think this will turn out differently? Ivalon wants respite, of course they do. But the pains—everyday, intermittent, acute—were bearable when they had Helo, because Helo believed them. He believed Ivalon when they said that none of the cures worked, he believed that their pain was something real and tangible, even when other doctors and people in their village said they must be exaggerating, for surely no one could possibly function in such distress. Helo would look to them, and roll his eyes in a shared understanding when others tried to pretend they knew how Ivalon lived. He always trusted all of Ivalon's testimony.

Helo cared for them, sometimes watering the garden and setting soup on the stove when the burdens of the day were too great. Sometimes he looked towards the future, helping them devise an irrigation system to bring water in from the river, and worked alongside them when they were able to work until the task was done. He helped them find equilibrium and gentleness with themself—acknowledging their needs and capabilities in equal measure. Helo would not have set them upon this road, would not have let Boram encourage them to risk it all on a fairytale, and even if Ivalon had truly wanted to do so, he would have walked by their side. Boram meant well, but he wanted to *fix* too much.

Ivalon hopes Eudia will return, but in their heart they know it will not turn out so well. They have seen too many like themself succumb to snake oil peddlers, slip quietly away from the world and into oblivion without anyone left to care. They make their way down to the water and watch the sun rise, beautiful and terrible, splitting the sky like a wound. If they could see the far side of the lake, they would see all the silver pouring down amidst its rising, the waterfall itself the knife that makes the cut.

The boat washes ashore, and still they wonder if they should get in even though they suspect that something terrible awaits on the other side. It would mean leaving all this behind so they do not have to return to their empty house and the mocking words of those who will disbelieve all this just as their pain has been disbelieved all their life. They grit their teeth, readying themself to step into the boat.

Typhania awakens, panicked, having succumbed to sleep when she should have held vigil. She races as best she is able, shouting as she sees Ivalon grab the oar to steady themself as they enter the wooden tomb of the boat. "Halt!" she cries, and in the misty distance Ivalon pauses.

They look about, confused, not having realized there was anyone else in this place. They despair, for surely it is another person come to tell them what to do without listening to what they know. They could pretend patience for Alaric because their interaction was so brief, and Eudia was just a chit, but now they are worn out. They cannot countenance a return home to the mocking of their demented tale, yet another example of their addled brains, and they are too weary to try to save another lost soul after the last three days. They need rest. Perhaps they will float upon this red lake forevermore, take their merry time making it to the fabled falls. They pretend they do not hear Typhania, as so many have not heard them, and they step into the boat, pulling the oar around with difficulty to push off from the shore.

"Halt, I said!" Typhania emerges from the reeds into the orange morning.

Ivalon sees them, laboring with a cane and yet still racing, still trying.

"The boat will come again tomorrow," they say wearily.

"You do not understand! It is a trap!" Typhania shouts.

"Of course it is," they say.

Typhania cannot help but laugh, even though she knows full well the stakes. "There is another option." She reaches out to grab the boat, trembling both from the effort of holding it in place, and for the way it punishes her for interfering with its magic, sending shocks into her hands. Ivalon watches as she grits her teeth and speaks despite the pain, and listens as she tells them all she knows of this place, of the god and the sorcerer's mercy, and the curse that prohibits speaking of it. "But you have asked for help and offered it," she explains. "And I am here to accept it, on behalf of the commune in which I live, if you are still willing. I am here to tell you that there are others who have done as you have, and have made a life here. We find it easier to be together with others who understand, who are willing to help and be helped in return. We hope someday to redeem this place, to find a way to break the curse and save all those who have found themselves upon its evil roads, but for now we help each other and take turns rescuing those we can."

Ivalon pauses, tears in their eyes. The oar seems to animate itself in their hands, urging them to push off, to push free from this mortal plane. Perhaps this woman is a trick, but in their heart they know that is not true. They know the truth to be harsh, but also kind. They do not need the fantasy of a cure, or the oblivion of escape. Even if there was an answer to all their other ails, there is nothing that will bring back Helo, and yet, Helo would not wish for them to join him, not yet. Ivalon does not need the mercy of the falls. They have lived and loved and plied their trade, despite and because in equal measure for all their long years, and they will continue to do so.

They take Typhania's hand, and the cane that she extends to them, and together they leave the bloody shores behind, disappearing into the space between the roads that brought them here, the roads that only the wounded tread.

Lynne Sargent

Lynne Sargent is a queer writer, aerialist, and holds a Ph.D in Applied Philosophy. They are the poetry editor at Utopia Science Fiction magazine. Their work has been nominated for Rhysling, Elgin, and Aurora Awards, and has appeared in venues such as Augur Magazine, Strange Horizons, and Daily Science Fiction. Their work has also been supported through the Ontario Arts Council. To find out more visit them at scribbledshadows.wordpress.com

This story came from a desire to write a fairytale that bucked traditional narratives of cure and disability-as-villainy.
I was incredibly inspired by Amanda Leduc's "Disfigured: On Fairy Tales, Disability, and Making Space," as well as Eli Clare's "Brilliant Imperfection". I specifically wanted to look at chronic pain because of its general intractability.
In this story, the "cure" is a misleading danger, pushed upon Ivalon by well-meaning but able-bodied friends, and each of the travelers is a victim primarily of ableism, rather than their conditions. The "happily ever after" instead of being a magical cure then gets to be the discovery of shared community and understanding.

Angharad ferch Truniaw

— by Tam Ayers

In the summer of her eighteenth year, Angharad ferch Truniaw declared that she would be leaving the small village of her birth and traveling east to seek her father's burial place. He had been slain in a great battle when she was small, along with most of the men of their village, and none of their bodies had been returned to their homes. Her mother wept and wailed all morning as Angharad filled her pack with what food their meagre stores could spare and strapped on her sword.

"I beg you, Angharad, do not go! If you are killed out in the wilderness, who will help me harvest the crops in the fall, and carry them to market?"

"I must go," said Angharad. "Do you not wish for Father to be buried in hallowed ground? And if I find Father's grave, perhaps I will find the rest of the men. Then our whole village may be at ease."

"Very well," said her mother, for she knew her daughter was a stubborn young woman and would not be swayed from her path. "Take this, at least. It was the first gift your father gave to me, and it may give you luck."

Angharad allowed her mother to put the small, plain silver ring onto the pointer finger of her left—and only—hand. "I shall return as soon as I am able," she promised, and kissed her mother's tear-soaked face.

*

She walked for several days, exchanging farm labour for hot meals and places to sleep at the cottages along the tightly packed dirt roads. At each residence, she asked if they knew where she might find the burial places of the men in her village, but she had little luck. One man, so old that his hair was nearly translucent and his skin was traced with blue veins, told her a story about a lord who had fought a great battle against the men of the neighbouring kingdom and, once he had defeated them, cut off their right arms and made a cairn of them. He could not tell her where the cairn of arms might be, or if the story were true. Angharad thanked him for the story with enough firewood to last him through the winter, and continued on her way.

On her fourth day of traveling, Angharad left the rolling farmland and entered the wild moor country beyond. She took her midday meal beside what might have once been a cottage but had since become a tumbled-down pile of stones. As she unwrapped her little bundle of cheese and dried meat, she heard hooves pounding on the ground. Out of the east rode a man in fine clothes on a beautiful white horse, its mane flying in the wind. Angharad stood and bowed. To her surprise, the man halted.

"Hail, lady," he said. "Hast thou seen any marvels on your travels?"

"I do not know what you mean by marvels, sir," said Angharad. "There are many kind people along this road, and I have seen a red kite flying in the skies, but I have not seen anything that might be truly called a marvel."

157

"Blast." He dismounted and rummaged in his saddlebags. "May I join you? I have ridden long and hard, and it would be nice to eat somewhere that is not my saddle."

"Of course," said Angharad.

The man sat beside her with a hunk of stale bread in his hands. He was not much older than she was, with green eyes and freshly tanned pale skin. Angharad pitied his meagre fare and gave him some of her dried fruit.

"Why are you seeking marvels?" she asked once they had finished eating.

"I want to prove myself to be a great warrior," said the man. "But I only ever seem to be making a fool of myself. When I last fought in a duel, I dropped my sword, and the man I was fighting spared me because he felt so sorry for me."

Angharad shoved a handful of fruit into her mouth to avoid laughing at the poor fellow. When she had finished chewing, she said, "I do not know if I can help you there. I am merely a farm girl seeking her father's grave, nothing more. Tell me, have you seen any cairns on your travels? Particularly cairns that may be made from human bones."

The man blanched and stared at her. "I have not seen any cairns of human bones, but there is one on the shores of Llyn Syfaddon. If you keep following this track, you will see it in about three days' time."

"Llyn Syfaddon? If you are seeking marvels, then you might wish to go there. The stories say that an afanc lives in that lake."

"I have heard the same stories." The man looked rather embarrassed. "I… er… I did not wish to be eaten by an afanc, so I did not seek its cave."

"That is understandable," said Angharad. She closed her pack and stood to leave. "I am glad to make your acquaintance, and I wish you well on your travels."

"Here." The man took a silk purple handkerchief from his tunic pocket and tied it around Angharad's right bicep. "For luck in your travels."

Angharad was surprised, but she still said, "Thank you, sir. I hope you will find many marvels, and none as terrifying as an afanc."

On the morning of the third day since she had met the young man, Angharad came across a party of young women going the same direction the young man had been riding. These women were dressed well, in white kirtles with gold belts, and all wore their hair loose.

"Hello, traveller!" they exclaimed when they saw Angharad. "Where are you going?"

"I am seeking the grave of my father," said Angharad. "Where are you traveling to? There is nothing much but moorland behind me."

The women giggled. One woman, with dark brown skin mottled with white patches and neatly twisted locs much longer than Angharad's own, said, "We are on pilgrimage, of a sort. We have heard that there are many young knights riding about these parts, and we wish to make their acquaintances." The other women giggled again.

"I have seen one such fellow," Angharad said. "He rode past me just three days ago, and though I am indifferent towards men and their looks, I am sure he was quite handsome. You might catch up to him if you continue to follow the road."

"Thank you for telling us," said the spokeswoman. "I hope you will find what you seek." She took a golden bracelet from her extensive collection and put it on Angharad's wrist with deft fingers. "For luck."

Angharad left the troop of women behind and soon crested the top of a hill. A great lake spread out before her in the valley below. This must be the one the young man had told her of. She descended the slope into the valley and walked with measured steps towards the shore.

It was not hard to find the cairn. A few paces from where the hill flattened out into shoreline, the reeds receded like trees before a glade to reveal a large domed structure of neatly placed blocks. Angharad had not believed the old man's story of a cairn of limbs, but she was still cautious as she ran a hand over the surface. Though she had never touched human bones before—only those of chickens or sheep—she was certain that this was stone. She walked its circumference with measured steps, her hand still touching the rough surface. There was no way to know who had been buried here.

A splash erupted from the lake. Angharad leapt away from the cairn, her hand going to her sword hilt. Something was swimming towards the shoreline. The story of the afanc came to her, and she backed up towards the cairn. It was said that the afanc was clever and strong. Surely it would be more than a match for a girl with no more swordcraft than the blacksmith's elderly father had been able to teach her.

The shape in the water grew closer, and Angharad resolved herself to action. She was not a coward; she was the daughter of a man who had fallen in a great battle. If she fled from an afanc, her father would surely be ashamed of her cowardice. She had to face it.

Angharad crept towards the shore and into the water, hoping it would not notice her movements. Her heart pounded in her throat. Water surged up as the form emerged from the water. Angharad leapt to strike.

A sudden geyser of water threw her backwards. That had not been one of the powers of the afanc in the story. This was something worse. She scrambled to her feet, sword in hand, and saw her foe for the first time.

It was a man. He was an ordinary sort of man, with the deeply tanned olive complexion and dark hair common among the farmers of Angharad's village. His beard was more grey than black, and deep lines were carved into his face, both from age and from blades. He was well-muscled in the same way that the few men with any sort of swordcraft left in their village were, an observation supported by the scars on his raised hands.

"What manner of sorcery was that?" Angharad shouted at him. "Who are you?!"

"I might ask you the same question," said the man. "I do not have anything of value, although you are welcome to look through my belt pouch." He gestured to a pile of clothes on the shore, which Angharad had not noticed in her determination to attack the supposed lake monster.

"I am not a bandit!" Angharad would have been more sheepish regarding her actions if she had not just been attacked with water. "I thought you might be an afanc, for I have heard that one lives in these waters."

"I am no afanc, and the one that was formerly of this lake is long dead." The man ploughed his way towards the shore. He had an odd, uneven manner of walking, as if his left side were much heavier than his right.

Angharad got out of his way and waited patiently while he shook himself off and pulled on his clothes. They were very plain, well-worn clothes, full of patches and neatly repaired seams. Over his hose went a pair of stiff leather and metal braces. One of the other girls in the village wore a similar brace due to what her mother claimed was a curse brought on by her husband cheating with their dairymaid, and what Angharad's mother said was just an accident of birth.

"Who are you?" she asked when he pushed himself to his feet.

"I am the hermit of this lake," the man said without looking at her.

"What sort of a hermit are you? Have you taken religious vows?"

"No, I have not. I am… I shamed myself long ago, and now I live alone."

Angharad wondered what kind of shame might force someone to choose isolation. "How long have you lived on this lake? Perhaps you can help me with my quest."

"I have lived here for sixteen years."

"Then you may know the information I seek. Who is buried in that cairn?" She gestured with her right arm.

"The fallen warriors of Deheubarth," said the hermit. "In a great act of hubris, they thought they might be able to pillage these lands until there was nothing left, but the king was not easily caught unawares. He slaughtered them as punishment for their actions."

Angharad gave him a hard look. "That is not the tale I was told. The men of Deheubarth were challenging a great tyrant, and he cruelly destroyed them."

"I am sure people will tell many different tales of that battle." The hermit stared at the cairn, a haunted look crossing his face.

"My father was among them."

The hermit stiffened.

"I wonder if you know if he was buried there," Angharad continued. "His name was Truniaw ap Gwestin, and he…"

"He was not buried there." The hermit did not look at her. "He alone was spared, for his mother lives under this very lake. She saved him, and he lived when the men he had led through Rheinwg did not. He was too ashamed to return home, for he knew the people of his village would assume that he had betrayed his comrades to the king of Rheinwg, because he was born there, and grew to manhood there."

"How do you know so much of him?" Angharad's hand returned to her sword. "I knew you were some sort of fairy-man; how else could you control the lake like that? What did you do with him, hermit?"

"I am sorry I stayed away so long, Angharad-fach. I did not want your—"

"I never told you my name, you—" Angharad froze with her hand still on her sword hilt.

The hermit—her father—looked at her, and his eyes were sorrowful. "It was a foolhardy choice. I know it was, and your grandmother has often told me so. But I could not bear to stain your reputations. What would the villagers have said if only I had come back? What would they have said of you?"

She balled her hand into a tight fist and tried very hard to steady her breathing. "You should have written, at least."

"Who would I have been able to give a message to? Few people come this way."

"I passed two parties of people on my way here," she snapped.

"They rarely come to the lake."

"Why would you think leaving us altogether would be better than coming home in shame?" Angharad was shaking so hard she thought her bones would rattle right out of her skin. "Why do you think so little of the villagers that you assume they would blame you?"

"Because they would be right to blame me." Her father looked towards the cairn. "It was I who gave our liege-lord the idea to come here, and it was I who led them. I thought he would merely learn not to boast of his prowess over others, not…"

"But why?"

"I was tired of him, Angharad." He turned back to her then. "I was tired of playing his games and fighting his battles, and I wanted a way out. I wanted a better life for you and for your mother, and—"

"It does not sound like you wanted something better for us," Angharad snapped. "It sounds as if you wanted something better for you."

She turned and marched away down the lakeshore until she reached a cluster of large rocks. There, she sat down and wrapped her arm around her knees. It was only then that she let herself weep. She had thought this journey would bring at least some sort of closure, but it seemed all she had to show for a weeks' travel was the knowledge that her father was… what? A coward? A traitor? A fool?

No, she did not think her father was a coward. Not really, anyway. The young man she had met that first day was a coward for not wanting to fight the afanc… but then again, was he? What was a coward? In all the old stories, men who fled battles were cowards, and men who rushed into them were heroes, even—and especially—if they died. In that case, her father, who had apparently sought out this battle in order to rid himself of a distasteful liege lord, might really be a hero. But then again, was it brave to goad a man into wasting the lives of his own men?

The uneven sound of slow, dragging feet roused her from her thoughts. She looked up to see her father approaching, a plate of what looked and smelled like fish stew in his hands.

"Go away." Angharad glared at him.

"It is getting late," he said, setting the stew down beside her rock. "There is room enough for you to sleep on the floor in my hut, if you will accept it."

"Why should I accept something like that from you?"

He sat on a rock beside her and stared out at the lake. The setting sun coloured the water red and pink. "You do not have to, Angharad. I understand why you would not want anything from me."

Angharad looked at the lake, too. The water was still, except for where tiny wavelets lapped against the shore. A family of ducks swam about the centre, occasionally dipping down into the water to catch fish.

"Does Grandmother really live under the lake?"

"Yes. Her and your uncles and aunts."

"Why?"

"It is a long story." Her father sighed. "Our father was not kind to her, so she took us and fled back to her home. I was the youngest and the slowest, and our father was able to catch me. He learned his lesson, but…" He spread his hands.

"So, you know what it is like. To be without a parent."

"I do, yes." He rubbed one hand over his beard. "I am sorry we must share that. I know I have been a fool, and I know also that I can never truly atone for abandoning you."

Angharad picked at the knot of the handkerchief the young man had given her until it loosened enough for her to pull it free of her arm, and wiped her face with it.

"Was that a token from someone back in the village?" her father asked.

"No. Well, it was a token, but from a young man I met along the road. He gave it to me for luck, though I am not sure it has worked." She showed him the bracelet and her mother's ring. "A lovely young woman gave this bracelet to me along the way, and Mam gave me your ring, both for luck as well. I thought I might stumble upon a great cache of gold with all the luck that has been wished upon me, but all I have come across is…" She trailed off and balled the handkerchief up in her fist.

"Was finding me not a stroke of luck?"

"It has certainly complicated things."

"Yes, I am sure it has." He put a hand on her shoulder. "Angharad, I would not want to make your and Ceinwen's life more challenging than it must already be. If you wish to leave me here…"

She looked at him in surprise. "Why would I do that? Mam will be overjoyed that you are alive. And, in any case, it means we will have someone else to help plow and harvest."

"So, I am merely a glorified farm hand to you."

Angharad began to protest, but she noticed a mischievous look in his eyes. "Da! Don't tease, or I really shall leave you behind."

He tousled her hair. "I would never."

They settled into a more comfortable silence. Finally, her father said, "It is a rather long way to walk, and I am not particularly quick on my feet."

"We need not rush back," said Angharad. "Perhaps we can purchase a horse. Perhaps that young man will lend us his. I doubt he is going to find any marvels: not where he was headed, at any rate."

Her father smiled. "You would be surprised, my dear."

Angharad looked at him. She had very little memory of his face from before he had left, as she had been too small to retain memories of any substance. All she did remember were small, inconsequential things: the feeling of his beard scratching her face, the smell of metal polish that had always seemed to hang about him, and the way he would pick her up and toss her into the air when he returned to their rooms in their lord's castle. She realized, with some shock, that he must not have been much older than she was now when he had gone off with his liege lord. It would have been hard to escape such a man, especially given the stories she had heard in the village. What was a young man with a limp and a little girl supposed to do in such a scenario?

"I would not mind sleeping on your floor," she said finally. "So long as you come home with me."

"Very well," said her father.

Angharad stood and helped him to his feet. Her father retrieved the abandoned bowl of stew, and together they walked back towards his little hut.

In the morning, they set out for home. Angharad spared one last look at the lake as they turned away towards the road. If her eyes were not mistaken, an elderly woman sat on one of the rocks in the centre of the lake. Angharad reached to tug on her father's tunic sleeve, but when she looked back, the woman had vanished. So, the tale of her lake-dwelling kin had not been so foolish after all.

At the top of the hill, they encountered the young man and his white horse. Riding behind him, as if she had been born to ride behind handsome young men in fine clothing, was the young woman who had given Angharad her bracelet.

"Well met!" called the young man. "Did you succeed in your quest?"

"In a way," replied Angharad. "I see you succeeded in yours, my lady."

The young woman grinned and winked. "My friends are quite jealous, for they will have to continue their search."

"I think I have tired of seeking marvels," the young man said. "Although, I may change my mind when I am older and more courageous."

"Do not worry so much about finding adventures," Angharad's father advised. "They are not worth much of anything."

"Sound advice!" The young man beamed, and the young woman waved, and they rode off to the east.

"I hope they will be happy together," Angharad said as they continued down the road. "He seems like a silly sort of man, but she seems quite kind."

Her father smiled and offered her his arm. "I hope they will be, too."

Tam Ayers

Tam Ayers is a music teacher by day and a writer of queer fantasy by night. He began writing at a young age and has pursued it throughout his life, delighting and amazing his friends, who also live in fear of the times he uses his power for evil and brings them great sorrow. He lives in St. Paul, Minnesota, USA, where he spends what time he has in between lesson planning biking around the local lakes and eating as much cheese as possible. This is his first published work.

The seed for this story came to me in the Welsh legend of Triunein Vagelauc, as recorded by the medieval writer Walter Map. I have retained the skeleton of that tale in Angharad's father's background, albeit with several name changes and embellishments. I was intrigued by the complicated themes of colonial power woven into many of the stories related by Map. While the portrayal of Triunein's fairy mother is likely intended to be frightening to Map's audience, it can also be read as a story of resistance to assimilation.
The fairy woman flees her husband's violent bridle and takes her fairy children back to where they came from, and it is the power of that connection that saves Triunein. I decided to take that theme of parents and children connected by marginalization and run away with it. Solidarity and understanding are powerful things!
Many, many thanks are due to my dear friends Eleanor, for her expert wisdom on Welsh and Welsh legends, and Steph, for her proofreading and encouragement.

The Girl & The Gum-Riddle

— by Ella T Holmes

It was a stark and warmish night when Amelia's sister brought the gum-riddle home with her. It burrowed into Claire's skin, raised and prickled it like the just-plucked flesh of a chicken, pilled it like Grandad's old tweed jacket; cooked her from the inside like the hot metal wire of a lightbulb; pocked her gums up like the bit of paper Amelia was meant to do her homework on but chose to stab over and over with her HB pencil instead.

She must have caught it at Sam's, mum said. They'd had a sleepover the day before, and wouldn't you know, Sam was sick before she asked if she could have friends over, and her mother didn't think anything of it. Claire had apparently caught it by the scruff and eaten it whole, Amelia thought. Look at the state of her!

Of course, by the time everyone knew Claire was sick, Amelia had fallen sick as well.

In her feverish delirium, she thought she could see Claire digging about in their dad's vegetable patch, discovering old bones riddled with the disease. Amelia was hot—so hot. She dreamed of wading through sand dunes, a real-life trip through her metallic-covered Egyptology book, then right into the maw of a dragon from the other book propped open on her bedside table. She didn't like swimming, but she was wet. Her dad said she was sweating too much. And she was sweating, watching Claire in her eight-year-old fury, digging up mummies in the garden and wrapping them both up in the old bandages till neither of them could breathe.

The gum-riddle took up residence in the spaces between her teeth, and unfurled itself down into the depths of her chest, like a hot and purring cat with no consideration for just how uncomfortable it might be for her if it rested across her lungs. Her gums split and her throat hurt, and she couldn't talk enough to tell it to bugger off, nor even to thank her mother for the chicken soup she made.

The gum-riddle looked Amelia in the eye and hissed at the salty dinner. Amelia did not eat.

The gum-riddle hacked up bile when the antibiotics she took washed down her throat, carried by warm honeyed tea; a push and pull that made her feel as if she were being drowned and dragged ashore again and again, emerging more tired each time.

Mum and Dad looked on. They brushed her hair back, helped her bathe, tucked her in. On and on for weeks, this gum-riddle stayed, until Claire's gum-riddle slunk away in the middle of a Wednesday night, leaving Amelia's all alone, with only Amelia's little body for company.

When it was clear the beast was here to stay, and the doctors didn't know how to treat it, her parents realised they had waited and trusted others long enough. They had always told Amelia and her sister that sometimes you have to go looking. Sometimes you have to fight battles. Sometimes you've got to do things on your own. They had just never thought it would ever come to this, a sick daughter and a dozen doctors with no clue. Thus they decided it was time to try something new.

They sent Claire to her grandparents' place, and took Amelia to a holiday house on the seaside, where they hoped they could coax the sickly beast out of her. Amelia's mother and father had been raised on old wives' tales, you see, and had superstitions about what lurked around the beach at night—sand ghosts, fish women who liked the taste of cartilage, little creatures that liked milk and knotting shoelaces together so one might fall. They didn't fancy summoning anything into the house—even good witches can do bad; even sand ghosts like the taste of flesh. But perhaps being here, amidst the otherworldly things, would be enough to bring the gum-riddle out? They could trap it in a box. Throw it into the sea.

Even with all these ideas, and even with that hope gripping their hearts, they were quite surprised when the gum-riddle opened its phlegm-yellow eyes and peered out at them from between Amelia's swollen tonsils. It got up and walked around—that was a good sign, surely!

But it walked straight through the cardboard box they dropped over it, leapt right out of the wooden crate they chased it into, and shredded the metal toolbox Amelia's father used as a last resort. It could not be trapped.

And it certainly did not leave.

It followed them when they returned home, and followed Amelia when she returned to school. Even as she regained some of her strength, and her cheeks regained a healthy ruddy colour, she tired quickly each day and kept complaining about the sores in her mouth. They were taking forever to heal, and every third day saw a new cluster or pustule. When she brushed, her gums would bleed and the sores would sting, and she'd cry herself to sleep on her parents' laps.

The gum-riddle trounced around as somewhat of a house cat, something invisible to others at school but smokey and intangible and very much there to the family. She was not contagious; the doctors had assured them all of that, if nothing else. But Amelia was exhausted and uncertain of how to be a kid now that the gum-riddle had become her constant, invisible companion, sapping her of energy and limiting her fun.

Children would come to school with winter agues, and Amelia would seem to catch them thrice-over at once, sickening so badly her chest would bubble and wheeze. They would come to school with coughs and colds, and Amelia would seem to catch them thrice-over as well, turning so poorly she would have to sleep sitting up in a recliner, a sheet laid over the top in a makeshift tent to help her breathe. Her parents kept her home, safe. She knew this and did not resent it, for home meant rest, and she was sorely tired, and tiredly sore. Though in the quiet moments, she imagined herself doing all the things she used to without a care, and missed it.

But Claire would return home with summer bags packed full and in need of washing, with a handful of pink tickets from the arcade, with swimmers on and her hair still dripping, and the same thing would happen; any illness or ailment that could be shared, the gum-riddle caught it and dropped it on Amelia's chest like a house cat might catch and deliver a house lizard, and that was the beginning of days, if not weeks, of worrying unwellness. The dream of her and her sister unearthing worm-riddled bones and wrapping each other in mummy cloths became something steady and reliable, its repetition a strange comfort. Some nights, Amelia could turn the garden into a forest, the bones into shining treasure.

It went on for months and months, and it just wouldn't do. Amelia's parents wanted Amelia back—the healthy one, the strong one, the whole one.

So they returned to the seaside, and cast aside all hesitance in summoning the witch they could only hope was truly good, and real.

They cut an onion in half, stuck the flats on the bottom of their daughter's feet, and secured the vegetable there with a pair of old woollen socks. They left the front door open, and a bowl of honeyed milk out on the deck for the little beach folk that might very well come visit. They even spun seven and a half times in front of their wood fireplace, clicked their fingers, and recalled the rhyme they had grown up on, for they would do anything, no matter how silly, to fix their daughter.

Good witch, bone witch,

A cauldron brew,

Eye blink, breath hitch,

Lady of Myrtle.

Seven turn dance, half a turn too,

I ask a potion, a spell from you.

"Isn't this stupid?" Amelia's father asked, pinching the bridge of his nose. He sagged down onto the old two-seater couch, a brown thing that had seen more years than he had. "We've lost it."

"Lost it utterly," Amelia's mother agreed, sitting beside her husband.

They held each other in the comfortable silence left by Amelia's peaceful sleep in the other room, and soon fell asleep under a shared blanket, clutching to uncertainty and hope and madness.

But of course, they were not mad.

They were desperate. And the Lady of Myrtle always comes to call in desperate times—it is one of the reasons they beheaded her all those centuries ago, this lady who was once called Marianne. A call to marriage she bluntly denied, and took up instead the call to the forest by the seaside. A call to needlework she couldn't fulfil due to her unreliable joints, and took up instead the call to wander. The men didn't like that one bit, and while she is still visited by nightmares of the axe, their displeasure has only fuelled her.

She poked the mother and father with the end of her magnificent wooden cane, prodded them wide awake. "The hour is late. I do not begrudge a midnight call, but I do ask a bit of hospitality in return."

Amelia's parents didn't know what to do at first, but once their minds had caught up with them, they leapt up to the kitchen and turned on the kettle.

A moment later they turned around as if now finally awake, the water climbing to a boil. "Who are you?"

"Who do you think?" The Lady spun in a knobbly-kneed, age-slowed, chronic-pained circle. "You did that seven and a half times, yes? Said the whole rhyme, too? My hearing has never been perfect."

"Ah." Amelia's mother looked half-dazed.

"So you're real, then," said Amelia's father. He took the kettle and set about making tea, his back turned.

"Have a seat—make yourself comfortable." Amelia's mother indicated for the Lady of Myrtle to take up a chair at the head of the small rectangular dining table.

"What is it you need from me?" the Lady asked when everyone was sat with steaming mugs of sugared tea in front of them. She added a third spoonful and stirred it without touching the spoon, which rather convinced the two sceptical adults that she was indeed the one they had summoned.

They glanced at each other. "Our daughter, Amelia," said the father.

"She's sick." Her mother's brow creased, deep like the crevices in the skin of a stringybark tree. "She keeps getting sick. It's the damned monster that's attached itself to her—it won't leave."

The Lady sighed, turning to the open door which allowed her to see Amelia's sleeping form. "And?"

"And," he spluttered. "What do you mean, and?"

"I mean," she said, "and what do you want me to do about it? You haven't actually asked me anything, and you have not once said please. I know all about your daughter, but I don't know what it is you wish me to do for her."

Amelia's mother clasped her hands. "Please, help us fix her. Make her better. Normal again."

"Fix whatever the beast has done to her," Amelia's father said, "and please take it with you. We don't want it in our house any longer. It's like my wife says—we just want to get back to normal."

"We'll repay you, of course…" The mother's tone suggested she had no idea what repayment would entail.

The Lady let them sit and stew in that uncertainty for precisely two minutes, during which she drank her tea and let her weary, loose-jointed bones settle more firmly into the chair.

"You are a witch, are you not?" asked the father, softer now. "The doctors say a bad flu or virus could kill her, but you can use magic to fix her."

"I am not a witch," The Lady said. "And I cannot fix her."

"But—"

"She is not broken, only different from what she once was."

"You—"

"Besides that, nobody can. It is not only beyond me, but beyond the laws of the universe." The Lady knew this, as she had long taken a keen interest in matters such as these: magic, cosmos, flesh, all of it, through the ages. She was, much to the assured displeasure of her long-dead foes, well-educated.

Everyone sat in silence. Amelia slept, and the gum-riddle blinked tiredly at the party at the table, no words shared between them for a handful of long, uncomfortable moments.

"Then what can we do?" her parents eventually asked, hands held. Worry knitted their brows and their fingers, made them lean against one another for support.

The Lady of Myrtle softened. "Do you love her?"

"Of course!" they said at once.

"Then you can do just that. Warm her heart, and keep it safe. Make sure she is comfortable, and that she can lean on you any time she needs. The world is more a disabling place than this illness, my loves. Shape your world so that it helps and fits her as best you can," she said. "One who cannot eat wheat, when offered alternatives, does not starve. One who cannot use their legs all the time, when given a chair and plenty of ramps, can move through the world. One whose bodily defence is weaker, when given a helping hand and protected from other gum-riddles and winter agues, will live a long and happy life. You may not like all that you have to do, and sometimes it may be difficult, but it is your responsibility, for she will never be able to keep herself safe as long as she lives with others. That is the great truth of this world: we all share it. We breathe the same air."

The Lady clicked her fingers, and the gum-riddle which had for many weeks perched on Amelia's chest sluggishly slid down to the floor, like a long shadow leaking down, down, down toward her feet, not yet letting go of the young girl. "I shall take the creature home with me. This, I can do for you. Come!"

And it went, as all such creatures do when the Lady calls, trading Amelia's chest cavity and the spaces between her teeth for the Lady's cloaked shoulder. The little girl would not grow sores any longer, nor would her gums weep.

The Lady looked at Amelia's parents once more. "This world is not built for people like her. You did not know this before, but now you do. What you do with this revelation will shape her life, your lives, and the lives of others for the better, should you choose." She raised her chin. It sounded like one of the heroic quests of old, the one knights she used to know went on to prove their mettle. But this was different. Truer. "Choosing means letting go of whatever normal is. Would you ever want Amelia to feel as though she is wrong?"

"We—No… Of course we…" Amelia's mother began. She looked down at her undrunk tea, now cool on the table, her cheeks stained red.

Scratching the gum-riddle on the underside of its smokey chin, the Lady sighed. "I was beheaded for my wrongness, but I am told humans have outgrown that particular activity."

"I'm sorry," they said in tandem, blanching and wide-eyed. "I can't even imagine…"

The Lady smiled, not for happiness or particular want to be kind, but because it was something of a trifling fact of her life now, and the reactions of others were so strong—oh my, you were beheaded? I can't believe it! That must have been terrible! It was, of course. Can a beheading be anything but? It turns out that yes, after hundreds of years, with more good days than bad and more friends than foolish foes, the memory blunted and turned somewhat trivial. That is what she wished for Amelia, a belonging that would allow her to flourish.

Cracking her neck to each side, the Lady exhaled long and slow. "You will be old in twenty years, and need a walking aid. You may lose your hearing. You may lose your memories and be unable to care for yourself. Your body will find it harder to fight off illness, just like Amelia's. Ageing is natural, yet what comes with it is considered— what?" She laughed. Amelia's parents swore her head rocked atop her shoulders, too loose. "Everyone is or will be abnormal! Doesn't that quite undo the very idea of normalcy?"

Blankets rustled in Amelia's room, and the Lady of Myrtle disappeared.

"Mum?" Amelia croaked. "Dad?"

As for what happened next, I will not tell you in any certain terms. Perhaps the Lady of Myrtle disappeared by turning seven and a half times herself, the gum-riddle happy on her shoulder, and Amelia was cared for and lived a long and happy life. Perhaps Amelia was consigned to a life shut in her home, a tower of a single story. You would have to look and listen to the world to learn if it has indeed changed for the better.

All the same, as it often is in stories: it was a stark and warmish night when Amelia's sister brought the gum-riddle home with her, and a stark and warmish night when it left.

— Ella T Holmes

Ella T. Holmes always dreamed of being a Mad Hatter, Trojan horse, or a cunning princess who is definitely not a witch but reality intervened. Fortunately, she's got a knack for escaping it.

Born and raised around Australia, Ella spends her time avoiding bush turkeys, and drinking enough coffee to bring down the moon. Her work has been published in or is forthcoming in Antithesis, Orca, and Macfarlane Lantern Publishing Seasonal Anthologies, among others. You can find her non-fiction work and newsletter over on Substack as 'ella has thoughts' and on socials as @ellatholmes.

For this anthology, I decided to tell a fantastical version of the illness I had at thirteen that left me immunocompromised. Doctors didn't know what was wrong, and I was sick for weeks, riddled with aches and pains and gum issues. To this day I still go through flares of this odd immune response, and it's like being visited by a stinky stray that is at once familiar and somewhat of a bothersome thing, but also has become so much a part of my life that I can't imagine my body being any other way. In light of the ongoing COVID pandemic, I also wanted to explore the idea that 'treatment' is communal, rather than some sort of magical injection. After all, we share this world, and it should be a safe space for all.

City of The Sun

— by Kara Siert

Gods, did people really dress like this? Meena squirmed in the faded green silk, silently cursing the puffed sleeves and endless ruffles. The ballgown might've been fashionable when her mother had worn it, but the sagging lace and moth-eaten fabric held little of its original charm.

Amma always claimed Meena looked just like her mother, sometimes even calling her "Norah." But Meena found it improbable she had received her mother's best features—green eyes, pale skin, and ash brown hair—without retaining any of her absent father's looks.

Even if Meena had inherited Norah's beauty, it was gone now. She knew her body by the dimples and marks the rot had left after eating away at her flesh. *I should be grateful,* Meena reminded herself. The rot had taken Elric's arm and Raya's eye, and from others the disease stole even more, consuming organs and limbs until nothing remained. At least Meena had all of her appendages and senses.

Still, the silk dress felt wrong. This was the most important day of her life, and she didn't even feel comfortable in her own clothes. She should have come to the tribunal in her short brown dress and green apron, with her gray woolen stockings and laced boots. But Amma had insisted she wear her "best," even if it was a decades-old ballgown that exposed all of the scarring across Meena's chest and arms.

Beside her, Elric fiddled with his empty shirt sleeve, kicking his heels against the tiled floor. They had been seated in a huge ballroom; despite the dusty chandeliers and cracked marble, Meena could still see beauty in the Lauritzan architecture, completely different from the wattle and daub huts of the outlands. She tried to imagine her mother in a place like this, wearing the floor-length gown when it was new, her hair pinned up with pearls and jewels… Before the rot had exiled them all to the outlands.

Now the Judgment House in each province was the only piece of Lauritza most non-citizens would ever see.

The room grew warm, and the ballgown felt heavy on Meena's skin. A hundred candidates sat in rows around her, while guards ushered in even more. Less than a dozen from this region would be chosen for Lauritza, and of those only a few would be granted Bronze Citizenship. *It's all or nothing,* Meena thought.

I'm not leaving Amma behind.

No one spoke above a soft murmur, but the nervousness in the room felt palpable. Some prayed while others practiced their blessings. One boy's gift took the form of a paintbrush and easel; he created vibrant landscapes of columned buildings and steam-powered airships, likely his version of Lauritza. Many were young, since the rot often affected children, but an older woman sat a few rows away holding three delicate orchids. Her blessing must allow her to nurture plants; no one in the outlands would be able to afford such rare flowers.

"What will you play?" Meena asked Elric.

"City of the Sun," he said, closing his eyes. Meena knew he must be focusing upon his blessing, drawing upon the remainder of the rot, forming it into something beautiful. A glimmering lute formed in place of Elric's missing arm; his remaining hand formed the chords while the lute plucked its own strings. He sang in clear, gentle tones—a folksong telling of a great heroine who won many victories, amassing such a following that she founded her own city. The people's love for her burned so brightly their city became the sun itself.

"You'll do well," Meena said. "Musicians are a popular choice."

Elric fixed her with a look. "You needn't use your gifts on me."

That was the trouble with blessings like Meena's; no one ever believed she was speaking honestly. She reached out and took his hand instead.

A girl in the first row was called through to the next room. The rot had withered one of her legs, and she used crutches to walk. In less than a minute, she reappeared, face downcast. Meena offered her a sympathetic smile, but the girl did not even look her way.

Slowly, the first row cleared, followed by the second. Of the dozens called, only one returned with a clockwork band around his wrist, marking him as a Lauritzan citizen. He was met with cheers, embraces, and barely hidden jealousy. Meena recognized the boy from school; the rot had weakened his stomach but given him an exceptional mind for mathematics. His acceptance surprised no one.

"Elric Khatz," a guard called out.

Meena gave his hand a squeeze. Then Elric had disappeared through the double doors, and Meena knew regardless of his outcome, she would be next.

Maybe I should've waited... spent more time learning about my blessing... Some spent years practicing their gifts. But the last few winters had been hard, and Amma was not growing younger. As soon as the blisters had been absent for a year, signaling the disease's dormancy, Meena had added her name to the list of outlanders awaiting the tribunal.

The doors reopened, and Meena looked up to see Elric, still carrying his lute. Meena waited for him to show the clockwork cuff that most certainly had been awarded him—but his cloak shifted, and Meena saw only his empty wrist.

Elric shrugged. "They have enough musicians. It's all right; the folks here would miss my music if I went away." He patted her shoulder. "Good luck, Meena. I'm sure you'll convince them."

"Meena Telessar," the guard called out.

Meena stood, following the guard into a long corridor. He hardly spared her a glance, but Meena stared at him. Cropped hair, passive eyes, broad shoulders… She supposed the guard looked like any of the outlanders if they shaved, bathed, and had their scars removed or limbs repaired, but he had lived in Lauritza all his life, free of the rot.

Meena found herself in an ornate room inhabited by the three individuals who would pronounce her fate. They sat behind a long table, all dressed in outlandishly impractical outfits—the woman's dress boasted so many ruffles Meena wondered how she was able to walk, and so many gauges and gears bedecked the men's bowler hats that surely they must be on the verge of falling off.

"Rogue Hammersmith and Cordelia Carmine, of the Baron class, and Storm Winchester, of the Viscount class," the guard announced.

"Oh my," the woman gasped. "Her scars…"

"They can be removed, Cordelia," a mustached man said. Hammersmith.

Meena stifled a laugh. *If they think pockmarks are bad, wait until they see Raya's eye.*

"Well, of course," Carmine said. "It's simply unfortunate they are so… prevalent." She sighed and removed a small brass object from her skirts. She turned a key, and a miniature set of blades began to whir, faster and faster. "All of this excitement has made me rather faint."

Meena stared at the clockwork fan. Lauritza must truly be the City of Perfection if something as simple as stuffy air could be cured with a tiny device. Meena had heard the stories—that no one was hungry, for the nobles provided food for all; missing limbs could be remade with clockwork; and simple illnesses could even be cured with alchemy. There was nothing Lauritza could not fix—except for rot, of course.

"Well," Winchester said, "go on. Show us your gift."

Meena glanced between the two men, trying to decide who would be most likely to listen. The mustached man already fiddled with his ruffled cuffs, so Meena turned to the viscount who had addressed her kindly.

"Citizen Winchester," Meena began, "may I see your pocket watch?" Every respectable gentleman carried a pocket watch—or so Amma had claimed. The viscount's brow wrinkled in confusion, and Meena swallowed, trying to calm the thumping of her heart.

Winchester removed a watch from his waistcoat. The golden cover portrayed an airship flying over a clockwork city, and a twirling gear represented each number upon the clockface.

"It—it's beautiful," Meena said. "Surely it must be a treasured possession."

Winchester nodded, and some of the tightness in Meena's chest relaxed, ever so slightly. It was always best to start with the truth. "Have you… ever considered selling it?" Meena asked.

Hammersmith frowned, while Carmine leaned forward, her lips pursed.

Winchester shook his head. "Absolutely not. I'd considered gifting it to my nephew, but I would never part with it otherwise."

Good, Meena thought. The other two Lauritzans had heard his refusal, which would prove her blessing's power. Meena closed her eyes, drawing upon the remainder of the rot, focusing on her emotions.

She forced herself to remember how it felt when the blisters had covered her body, when they had grown in her throat. When Amma had spooned water into her mouth, and still it had burned. *Amma, begging her to eat, to not let go. Amma promising that if only Meena could endure, the gods would bless her.*

Yes, Meena thought. I remember. Then she took a deep breath and asked, "Would you consider giving your watch to me?"

"What an outrage!" Hammersmith slammed his gloved hand upon the table. "Even if you were a citizen, you would never speak to a viscount in such a manner. I—"

Carmine murmured something in his ear, and Hammersmith quieted.

Winchester's eyes locked with Meena's, his mouth turning downwards as if he were concentrating deeply.

Remember, Meena told herself. *Amma, telling her how Mama had died... How the rot had eaten her whole body.* Amma had been certain the gods would bless Norah for enduring such a tribulation, but they saw fit to take all of her instead.

Winchester closed his pocket watch slowly.

When she was young, Meena had asked what her mother had looked like. Amma had wept because her last memories were cruel. *Yes, I remember*, Meena thought. *I know what you have taken from me.*

The viscount held out his pocket watch, extending it towards Meena. Then Carmine's fan sputtered, and Winchester blinked and glanced away, breaking their connection. "Cogs and whistles!" he cried, looking down at his hand. "What is happening?"

Please, Meena thought. *Let it be enough.* Surely they could see her voice's power. Surely, they would choose her.

Carmine gasped. "Oh, how thrilling! A bewitcher!"

Winchester shook his head and returned the watch to his pocket. "When did your gift become evident?" he asked.

"During the blains stage," Meena said. "After four seasons of blisters, I discovered the ability of persuasion. When I fell into the trance stage, my gift grew as I learned to understand it."

"Are you able to convince hostile individuals?" Winchester asked.

Meena hesitated. "I believe, over time, I could learn."

"I don't like it," Hammersmith announced. "What's going to stop her from running amok in Lauritza, conning citizens out of their watches and jewels?"

A laugh erupted from Carmine's throat. "Don't be ridiculous. Gifted citizens are always made *productive* in society."

"Poor child," Winchester murmured. "Life has not been kind to her. If we cleaned her up, repaired her skin… She would be a grateful citizen indeed. A powerful reminder to Lauritzans of all that the nobles provide for them."

Hammersmith cleared his throat. "With respect, Lauritza has no need for charity cases. The city demands singing, dancing, and music—entertainment is wealth, Storm."

Carmine adjusted her fan, breathing in the cool air. "She has potential. Think of the political uses! Perhaps she could sway the populace to support a particular candidate or secure funding for a worthy cause. Turn her away, and we could destroy a future that will never come to pass without her blessing."

Hammersmith sighed. "This is why you'll never become a viscount, Cordelia. Do you forget our ranks are based on the *successes* of our candidates? You speak of hypotheticals and possibilities—everything but practicality."

I'm still here! Meena wanted to shout. They spoke as if she were a bruised apple at the marketplace, as if they did not hold her—and Amma's—lives in their grasp. Was this how they had spoken of Elric? They had heard his music and seen his gift, then sent him away without another thought. Amma had been given the blessing of comfort; she'd never bothered presenting herself to the tribunal, knowing they would see no use in such a gift. Meena had always been glad for her grandmother's soft embraces and gentle words, yet it seemed Lauritza offered no compassion without expecting profit in return.

Hammersmith and Carmine continued arguing, Winchester quietly interjecting. It seemed unfair that after Meena had spent years with burning blisters and broken skin, praying for a blessing, her future depended on three nobles who did not even know her.

Winchester cleared his throat. "Very well," he said. With a look at Carmine, who nodded, the viscount turned back to Meena. "This tribunal has elected to grant you an Iron Citizenship." He motioned towards a guard, who stepped forward with a clockwork bracelet. Winchester removed a bronze pen from his pocket, engraving Meena's name upon the band. "This mechanism is nontransferable and will permit you entrance to the city."

"And my grandmother?" Meena asked.

Carmine's brow creased ever so slightly. "I'm afraid we have limited Bronze Citizenships to offer. Bringing entire families to Lauritza is costly, and such an act is reserved for those who have the most potential—" Hammersmith shot a look in her direction—"to add to Lauritza."

"But—but I can't leave her." Meena's stomach twisted. She should be happy—overjoyed. Instead, tears formed at the corners of her eyes.

"It's what she would want," Winchester said, holding out the bracelet.

"No," Meena whispered. "Amma—she was born in Lauritza, she and my mother both. It was their home."

"Lauritza was everyone's home once," Hammersmith muttered, his voice gruff.

This is what your mother wanted. Meena heard Amma's voice in her head, felt her wrinkled hands upon her own.

"Please." Meena looked up at Winchester, trying to focus. Her gift was not nearly powerful enough, but she had to try. Meena thought of her mother, suffering in their apartment in Lauritza. Amma said that Norah had hidden the pregnancy—and the blisters—for eight months, refusing treatment in hopes of delivering Meena before they were taken away. And gods, she'd almost made it. Meena thought of her mother and grandmother, exiled from all they knew. *Remember.*

"No," Winchester said. "There are potions to help you forget, if you wish. Go and say your goodbyes; the airship leaves at six tomorrow morning." He grabbed Meena's wrist, snapping the cold metal against pockmarked skin.

*

Meena found herself at home, staring through the dirty window at Amma, trying to memorize every detail—her thinning gray hair pulled into a bun, her bony fingers and rounded shoulders as she hunched over the loom, and her worn skirts with ragged hems.

Norah had died shortly after Meena's birth, and Amma had raised her. *This was going to be my chance to take care of you, Amma.* And yet it had not been enough; her gift had not been enough. *She* had not been enough.

Meena pushed the door open, and when Amma's gray eyes fell upon the iron bracelet, she breathed a sigh so deep it seemed to travel through her entire body. "Oh, thank the good gods."

"No, I—" Meena didn't know how to begin. "They—they only gave me an Iron Citizenship. I can't—" The words wouldn't form. "I can't take you with me." Meena buried her face in her grandmother's shoulder.

"Oh, child," Amma murmured. "It's all right. Lauritza has no need for an old woman." She pulled away, looking Meena in the eyes. "Go and see if my favorite tea shop is still open. Cogs and Chamomile, I think it was called. Order a Perfect Brew and think of me."

Meena shook her head. "I don't want to leave you." As she reached for Amma's hand, her grandmother's sleeve slipped away to reveal a shock of bright red marks. Before Meena could react, Amma had already covered her arm.

"Just a little rash," she said, offering up a smile.

"No." Meena's voice shook. She knew those blisters and their sharp acidic smell; the weeping, oozing wounds; and the brightness of red, stark against wan skin. But it couldn't be. Once a person was blain-free for a year, the contagious blisters never resurfaced.

"Gods, Amma. How? You—you said…" They had all been sent to the outlands. Only Meena's father, a Baron Citizen, had been allowed to remain in a sanatorium. Meena shook her head. "You never had the rot. You left with Mama so she wouldn't be alone."

Amma took Meena's hands, squeezing gently. "And the best years of my life I have spent with you. See, it was meant to be this way; the gods spared me the rot for so many years. Now go to Lauritza, child, and do good there."

Meena glanced around the hut, spying the loom in the corner and the sparse food they were storing for winter. "The rot will only grow worse. You'll need someone to care for you. How long have you known? How long have you been hiding this from me?"

Amma shrugged. "The blisters appeared only a season ago. Or perhaps…" Her voice trailed into silence. "Perhaps two seasons. Or a year. I… don't remember now."

"A year!" Meena sank down at the table, running a hand over her face. "You're already in the second stage, then. The blisters should be everywhere. I don't understand…"

"I'll be all right, Norah," Amma said.

"I'm not Norah!" The words exploded from Meena's mouth. The hut felt stifling, and she shoved at the ballgown's lace, trying to calm herself. In her haste, the aged fabric tore. "I'm not Mama. I'm not your Norah—I'm *Meena!*"

"Meena," Amma repeated slowly. "Well, of course."

The rot… Meena breathed out, trying to calm herself. *It's not on her skin—it's in her mind.* "Amma, I'm not—I *can't* leave you."

"You must." Amma's voice was fierce. "It's what your mother would've wanted."

But what about what I want? Has anyone ever asked what I *want?* Meena wanted to scream the words at Amma, but she held them back, burying them deep in her chest.

"I did not sacrifice so that you could stay here," Amma said. Her hands, when she wrapped them around Meena, were gentle. "Go to Lauritza. Go home."

*

The sun peeked over the horizon as Meena crept out outside, her simple brown dress rustling against her ankles. She was glad to be wearing her boots and apron again; she felt more like Meena and less like Norah.

As she stepped into the street, Meena caught the soft strums of a melody. Elric appeared from a doorway, his lute glowing in the faint light. "Hullo!" he called. "I thought I'd see you off. Once you're in Lauritza, maybe you can even put in a good word for us." He winked at her. "With that voice of yours, I bet you could do a lot of good. Don't fret over leaving—I'll look after your amma." He grinned and began to play. *And in that city, she built and built, and in that city, she shone and shone, and in that city…*

Meena lost herself in his music until she realized they'd already reached the dock. A crowd of outlanders had gathered, along with the barons and viscount. A huge airship hovered in front of them, a clockwork dance of spinning gears and steam vents. As guards ushered the new citizens aboard, Meena glimpsed velvet seats and automaton butlers, satin pillows and trays of delicacies.

"Take care of yourself." Elric patted her on the shoulder before joining the onlookers.

"I—" Meena glanced down at her wrist. It seemed silly that such a small item would grant her access to an entirely new world. She looked behind her at the ramshackle huts with crumbling exteriors, a drab landscape of poverty and sickness. Ahead of her, the airship beckoned, its open door inviting her inside. *I'm sorry, Amma.*

"Citizen Meena?" a guard asked, checking her bracelet. "Very well, you may embark."

Meena's boot stepped onto the gangplank. She could hear the faint chords of Elric's music, ringing out from the crowd, a song to see her off. *And in that city, they sang and sang, and in that city, she reigned and reigned.*

Remember. Could she really allow Amma to become a memory? When Meena called upon the rot and reached for her deepest emotions, would she see Amma's and Elric's faces? Meena was not certain she could bear that, even if she were living in Lauritzan riches. *Remember.* Amma had left the City of Perfection for Meena, but she had always said the best years of her life had been with her. Would Lauritza truly be perfect without Amma there too?

Meena ran her finger over the iron cuff, touching the place where her name was engraved. *Citizen Meena.* Then she stopped, turned, and walked back to the barons and viscount. "With respect, I—" Meena grappled with the mechanism until it clicked open, the cuff releasing her hand. "All my life, someone else has decided for me. I did not choose to be cast out of Lauritza or ravaged by the rot, and I could only pray for my blessing. But today, *I* will choose. And I… I do not wish to go to Lauritza."

The baroness gasped, and Hammersmith frowned deeply. "What are you saying?" he demanded. "Do you not understand what we are offering you?"

"I understand," Meena said, meeting his gaze. "I understand you wish to take me to the clockwork city and remake me to be like you. But I am not broken, and I do not need you to fix me."

"The impudence!" Carmine whispered, as if the words were too terrible to speak any louder.

Winchester fixed Meena with a look. "You would cast aside your future for what—an old woman? A friend?"

"Her name is Amma," Meena said. "And his name is Elric."

Carmine clutched her fan, her cheeks growing red. "The girl is throwing away her potential."

Winchester sighed. "Cordelia, leave her be. She is young, foolish, and pitiable. The girl will live long enough to regret her mistakes and remember this moment forever." He took the bracelet from Meena, stuffing it into his waistcoat pocket. "We would have done well. You could've had perfection, child."

The nobles all turned away from her, striding towards the airship.

"We exist!" Meena shouted at their backs. "We always have, and we always will. You can try to erase us while hiding away in your 'perfect' city. But one day we will build our own city, and it will shine more brightly than the sun."

The door closed, the three nobles disappearing from view. With a great belch of steam, the ship lifted into the air, a dozen lights flickering inside. Meena thought she saw a silhouette in the window, watching her.

"Were you using your blessing?" Elric asked, appearing at Meena's side.

"No," she said. "That was the truth."

Together, they watched the airship sputter into the sky, growing smaller and smaller until enveloped by clouds. The onlookers wandered away until Meena and Elric were alone, standing at an empty dock while the sun rose before them, rays of light streaming across the horizon in pinks, purples, and blues.

"Now," Elric said, "tell me more about the city you wish to build."

Kara Siert

Kara Siert is a Chinese-American author who began crafting stories at the age of four, although they were rather nonsensical. She is passionate about using fantasy to explore themes of mental health, disabilities, and platonic relationships… but that's assuming she's actually writing and not making mood boards, playlists, or talking to her friends on Discord. Kara also dabbles in trying new baking recipes, adding books to her bookshelf that she'll forget to read, and making colorful digital art. She currently resides in the Appalachian mountains with her beloved husband and son.

Many stories explore illness and death, romanticizing our mortality and finding "inspiration" in others' struggles. Survivorship is much less exciting — it's hospital anxiety, follow-up appointments, and missing caregivers who have become like family. As a childhood cancer survivor, I had to learn to make my own choices when every other decision had been made for me, casting off society's projections and opinions to find a new way forward. Over the past two decades, I'm learning to accept both the body I now inhabit and everything that has been done to keep me living. When my son was born prematurely, I heard echoes of familiar themes. Dour futures were painted when I only wanted someone to give us a chance, to offer us a bracelet to the Golden City. I wanted to shout, "We exist!" Tales of survivorship may not be tragic or inspirational, but our stories of resiliency and hope deserve to be told.

Acknowledgements

This anthology has been a true adventure in collective input, creativity, and support. Calling it "magical" almost feels like doing a disservice to everyone's hard work and generosity, but sometimes things do indeed feel like a dream come true.

Thank you to Ellen Forget for working hard to bring us a braille file of this anthology.

I can't thank each of the contributors enough for their willingness to submit, donations, work on edits, thoughts, and input on design decisions. I would also like to extend my gratitude to those who got in contact with me throughout the process, who offered time and labour that goes beyond anything I could have hoped for. Without all of you and all of your generosities, this anthology would not exist!

I'd like to thank my first readers who helped make the story selection process less impossible (everyone is so talented!), the group chat for helping me work out why I wanted a comma where it didn't technically need to go (the answer is *prosody*), and my cat Mr. Bingley for keeping me company while I worked (but not for trying to use my keyboard as a pillow).

I hope this anthology is but the first of many.

Love,
Ella.